SCIENCE
FOUNDATIONS

Viruses

SCIENCE FOUNDATIONS

SCIENCE
FOUNDATIONS

Viruses

PHILL JONES

CHELSEA HOUSE
An Infobase Learning Company

Science Foundations: Viruses
Copyright © 2012 by Infobase Learning

Chelsea House
An imprint of Infobase Learning
132 West 31st Street
New York, NY 10001

Library of Congress Cataloging-in-Publication Data
Jones, Phill.
  Viruses / by Phill Jones.
      p. cm. — (Science foundations)
  Includes bibliographical references and index.
  ISBN 978-1-60413-341-7 (hardcover)
  1. Viruses—Juvenile literature. 2. Virus diseases—Juvenile literature. I. Title.
  QR365.J66 2011
  579.2—dc22   2010047648

Chelsea House books are available at special discounts when purchased in bulk quantities for businesses, associations, institutions, or sales promotions. Please call our Special Sales Department in New York at (212) 967-8800 or (800) 322-8755.

You can find Chelsea House on the World Wide Web at
http://www.infobaselearning.com

Text design by Kerry Casey
Cover design by Alicia Post
Composition by EJB Publishing Services
Cover printed by Yurchak Printing, Landisville, Pa.
Book printed and bound by Yurchak Printing, Landisville, Pa.
Date printed: October 2011
Printed in the United States of America

10 9 8 7 6 5 4 3 2 1

This book is printed on acid-free paper.

All links and Web addresses were checked and verified to be correct at the time of publication. Because of the dynamic nature of the Web, some addresses and links may have changed since publication and may no longer be valid.

Contents

Introduction to Viruses

Humans have tried to understand the nature of diseases for thousands of years. Knowledge about a disease can inspire methods for treating the illness and measures for avoiding the illness. For a long time, doctors thought that some unseen thing in the air brought disease. The invention of the microscope revealed the existence of **bacteria**. The presence of the tiny life forms suggested a cause of diseases that spread from one person to another. Then, scientists proposed that some infectious diseases were caused by agents smaller than bacteria. These agents were too small for the microscope. They were almost invisible.

THEORIES ABOUT DISEASE: FROM BAD AIR TO VIRUSES

Doctors used to blame bad air for causing disease. Hippocrates, perhaps the greatest doctor of his time, wrote a theory of disease in his book, *On Airs, Waters and Places* (400 B.C.). In it, he suggested a connection between disease and poorly drained land that emitted foul air. Vapors, also called miasma, caused disease. Over the years, others expanded the miasma theory of disease to include vapors given off by rotting bodies and vegetable matter. By the second century,

A LONDON BOARD OF HEALTH HUNTING AFTER CASES LIKE CHOLERA

Figure 1.1 An 1832 cartoon called *Sniffing for Cholera* depicts the miasma theory.

the foul-smelling breath of ill people had been added to the list of disease-spreading vapors. The nineteenth century brought crowded European cities with little or no sanitation. The cities had a lot of bad air. The constant spread of many diseases among city dwellers seemed to confirm the miasma theory.

Doctors and nurses urged that hospitals must be clean to purge miasma from the buildings. They promoted cleanliness, good ventilation, and the wide spacing of beds to separate ill patients. Engineers paid attention to the miasma theory when they built closed drainage and sewer systems. Along with garbage collection and public baths, the fears of foul air led to improved public health. The miasma theory sparked a sanitation revolution. Yet the revolt occurred for the wrong reason. Infectious disease was spread by something other than bad air.

After the invention of the microscope, some doctors suggested that small life forms might provide the answer to disease. In the eighteenth century, Scottish doctor Sir John Pringle wrote that microbes, rather than bad air, might explain how diseases are spread. In 1840, German physician Friedrich Gustav Jacob Henle argued that infection by microbes was a major cause of disease. London doctor

Figure 1.2   London doctor John Snow traced the source of a cholera outbreak in the Soho district of London, England, in 1854.

John Snow not only argued that biological agents caused disease but also showed that miasma did not spread one particular disease.

Within the first 10 days of September 1854, cholera killed about 500 people in London. According to rumor, it was miasma that spread cholera. People pointed to houses that had been built on land used to bury plague victims a century earlier. Miasma oozed from the old graves into the homes. Snow did not believe in the miasma theory. But he decided to test the rumor. Snow mapped cholera deaths that had occurred in one part of London and saw that the deaths were not located in areas of the old burial grounds. He thought that cholera might be spread by something in water.

Snow walked door to door to learn which water companies supplied water to each house. Two companies had supplied water during an earlier cholera outbreak. Both companies had obtained water downstream of an area often contaminated by sewage outlets. In 1852, one of the businesses—the Lambeth Company—had moved its waterworks upstream and away from sewage pollution. During the 1853–1854 cholera outbreak, Snow correctly predicted fewer deaths in households that used the Lambeth Company's water. He also found that the largest cluster of deaths and cholera cases had first occurred near a public water pump located on Broad Street. The doctor persuaded the government to remove the pump handle on the Broad Street water pump. The number of cholera deaths decreased. Something in the water had spread cholera.

A decade after Snow showed that bad air did not cause cholera, French chemist Louis Pasteur proposed his germ theory of disease. He suggested that some diseases are linked to microscopic pathogens. The germ theory differed from the miasma theory in two important ways. First, the germ theory called for a biological agent as the cause of disease. Second, the bad air of the miasma theory could inflict many types of diseases. However, the germ theory required a link between one particular type of biological agent and one particular type of disease. For example, one microbe causes cholera, but it does not cause the plague, dysentery, or other illnesses.

German physician Robert Koch proved the germ theory. He showed that one type of bacteria caused the cattle disease anthrax and that another type caused tuberculosis in humans. He also devised four steps for proving that an infectious agent produced a particular disease. Koch's method applied to animal diseases has the following steps:

1. Show that the biological agent is present in every case of the disease.
2. Isolate the agent from an infected animal and grow it in the laboratory.
3. Infect a healthy animal with the agent cultured in the laboratory to produce that same disease.
4. Isolate the same agent from the experimentally infected animal.

Subsequently, scientists followed Koch's procedure to identify the causes of many infectious diseases.

By the 1890s, scientists assumed that bacteria produced most infectious diseases. Sometimes, though, they could not isolate the agent that caused a particular illness. In 1892, Russian botanist Dimitri Ivanovski showed that something other than bacteria inflicted a disease in tobacco plants. The agent that infected the plants slipped through ceramic filters that had pores fine enough to retain bacteria. Whatever infected the plants was quite small. Six years later, Dutch scientist Martinus Willem Beijerinck showed that the tiny disease agent could be passed from one tobacco plant to another. He suggested that the infectious agent reproduced itself within plant cells. Beijerinck called the agent a *soluble living germ*. It soon became known as a **virus**.

The popular use of filters to isolate bacteria revealed the existence of many filter-passing agents that could be linked to diseases of plants and animals. In 1909, researchers showed that a filterable agent produced poliomyelitis. Polio was the first human disease found to be caused by a virus. Scientists soon discovered that some viruses even attacked bacteria. French-Canadian scientist Félix d'Hérelle called these viruses *bacteriophages*, or "eaters of bacteria."

By the end of the 1950s, researchers had learned about the physical features of viruses. Viruses contain a molecule of **deoxyribonucleic acid** (DNA) or **ribonucleic acid** (RNA) that has coded instructions for making **proteins**. A protein is a molecule that carries out many functions required to sustain life. A virus protects its DNA or RNA within a shell of proteins. To reproduce, a virus must

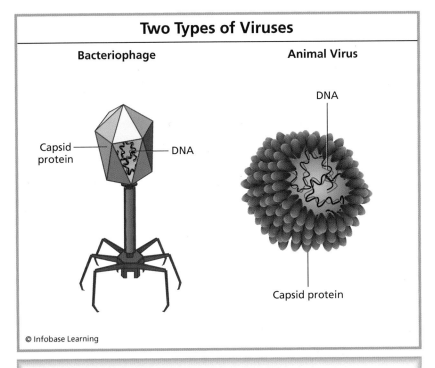

Two Types of Viruses

Bacteriophage

Animal Virus

DNA

Capsid protein —

— DNA

Capsid protein

© Infobase Learning

Figure 1.3   Viruses depend on the host cell that they infect to reproduce. In their simplest form, outside a host cell, they consist of only DNA or RNA, surrounded by a capsid protein (protein coat).

invade a cell and force the cell to make new viruses. A virus is thus a tiny **parasite**.

WHERE DO VIRUSES COME FROM?

Viruses can be found in water, in the ground, in the air, and frozen in polar ice. They cover the planet. Nobody knows the origin of viruses. However, scientists have proposed many theories. Astronomer Sir Fred Hoyle suggested that viruses travel through space and descend upon Earth, but most scientists believe that radiation would destroy any viruses drifting in the vacuum of space. Another theory is that RNA molecules developed the ability to reproduce when Earth was very young. Cells evolved billions of years ago, and they might have been parasitized by these reproducing RNA

Wrestling with a Virus

The price for competing in contact sports usually includes sore muscles and bruises. Players accept this consequence. Yet contact sports may also come with a hidden cost: a long-lasting viral infection called *herpes gladiatorum*. Herpes Simplex Type 1 virus causes the disorder. Skin-to-skin

(continues)

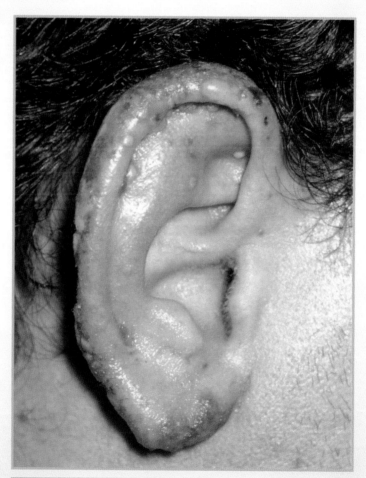

Figure 1.4 The ear and other exposed areas of the face are common locations to find Herpes Simplex Type 1 blisters.

(continued)

contact transfers the virus from an infected person to a healthy person. The infection appears as clusters of blisters on the head, neck, arms, legs, or trunk. *Herpes gladiatorum* is very contagious due to the virus-filled blisters. After the blisters heal, the virus may quietly wait in nerves for a long time. The viruses can activate to create a new set of sores.

High school wrestlers have had to battle *herpes gladiatorum* for years. In 1988, infections broke out among three Wisconsin high school wrestling teams. Researchers announced an outbreak in 1989 among 175 high school wrestlers who attended a training camp. Sixty wrestlers had viral infections. The Minnesota State High School League suspended wrestling programs in 2007 after 10 teams reported 24 cases of *herpes gladiatorum*. Lessons learned from previous outbreaks enabled doctors to prevent widespread infection among wrestlers. Recommended measures to prevent or limit an outbreak include the education of trainers and athletes about *herpes gladiatorum*, routine skin examinations before wrestling, barring wrestlers with suspicious skin lesions, and thorough cleaning and disinfecting of all equipment.

Typical American wrestling is not the only contact sport that can transmit herpes virus. In rugby, a *herpes gladiatorum* infection is called *scrumpox*, named for the scrummage play that requires close contact between players. Sumo wrestlers also risk infections. In 2008, scientists reported that sumo wrestlers in Japan had been infected with a new, deadly type of the herpes virus and that two sumo wrestlers had died from their infections.

molecules. Yet another idea is that a part of primitive cells evolved the ability to reproduce itself and became a parasite of the cell. Some scientists propose that devolution, not evolution, might explain the appearance of viruses. Viruses might have devolved from

Frozen Viruses

A virus called *tomato mosaic tobamovirus* is very rugged. It can be found in plants, dirt, oceans, and even fog and clouds. Floating on air currents, the virus has spread across the globe. Scientists wondered if the virus had drifted to the Arctic, where it became frozen in ice. To explore this possibility, they traveled to Greenland to obtain ice fragments from various depths. Back in the laboratory, they tested the ice for the presence of the virus. They found 15 different types of the virus in ice samples dating from less than 500 years old to about 140,000 years old.

The discovery of the first virus preserved in ancient ice raises a chilling prospect. As global warming melts Arctic ice, ancient viruses may be released into the environment.

bacterialike life forms, becoming so simple in structure that they survived by parasitizing cells.

No matter where viruses came from, they are here to stay. They infect plants and animals around the globe. They inflict human diseases on every continent—diseases that cost millions of lives. They constantly challenge human ingenuity to find new ways to defeat the tiny parasites.

Cell Hosts for Viruses

A virus cannot make a copy of itself. It lacks the materials to produce new viruses. A virus cannot even make the materials for new viruses. Viruses rely upon other forms of life to reproduce. They are parasites. To reproduce, a virus infects a cell and takes over the host cell's functions to produce molecules that form new viruses. Before exploring how a virus hijacks a cell, it is helpful to examine how a cell normally functions.

ANATOMY OF AN ANIMAL CELL

An animal cell is covered by a membrane that retains the cell's contents. The inside of a cell contains a jellylike mix of water and proteins called *cytosol*. If the cell membrane becomes damaged, cytosol will ooze from the cell. A loss of cytosol disrupts the cell's functions required for its survival.

Within the protective cell membrane, a cell is organized like a factory. A factory is divided into departments with different functions. One department may oversee the company's finances, another takes care of hiring, another department maintains a computer network, and another manufactures a product. Similarly, a cell is divided into compartments that perform different jobs required for its survival. Factories have walls and cubicles to separate different functions. Cells have membranes that divide tasks among small

Structure of an Animal Cell

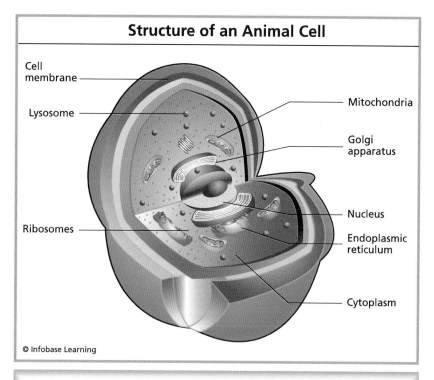

Cell membrane

Lysosome

Ribosomes

Mitochondria

Golgi apparatus

Nucleus

Endoplasmic reticulum

Cytoplasm

© Infobase Learning

Figure 2.1   Because they don't have cell walls, as plant cells do, animal cells can take on a variety of shapes.

organlike structures called *organelles*. A cell, like a factory, manufactures products, such as proteins, which are molecules that carry out many functions required to sustain life.

The following five organelles play vital roles in the synthesis of proteins:

- **Mitochondria** are jelly-bean-shaped organelles that process molecules obtained from food to supply energy to the cell. They power protein synthesis.
- The **endoplasmic reticulum** is a collection of folded membranes where the cell synthesizes many proteins.
- **Golgi bodies** are disk-shaped structures that aid in the delivery of the cell's proteins. Certain proteins are modified in Golgi bodies to prepare the proteins for export outside the cell.

- **Lysosomes** digest waste products created by the cell and debris that travels inside the cell. These organelles break down complex chemicals to simple chemicals that the cell can use to make new products. A lysosome is part of the cell's recycling center.
- The **nucleus** is the cell's command center. It stores genetic material that instructs the cell how to make certain proteins.

Just as a cell has an outer cell membrane, a membrane called the *nuclear envelope* surrounds the nucleus. The nuclear envelope separates the nucleus from other parts of the cell. The inside of an animal cell has two basic parts: a nucleus and **cytoplasm**. Cytoplasm is simply the cytosol and organelles found outside the nucleus.

A nucleus cannot be totally isolated from the cytoplasm. After all, a nucleus is a cell's command center. The nuclear envelope has pores that allow certain molecules to move from the nucleus to the cytoplasm. These molecules pass on instructions from the genetic material to the protein-making machinery. An animal's **genome**—the genetic material that resides in the nuclei of an animal's cells—contains the complete set of instructions for the animal's body.

The instructions of the genetic material are stored in deoxyribonucleic acid (DNA) molecules. Typically, DNA in an animal cell nucleus can be found in chromatin, which is a mixture of DNA and proteins. Under the microscope, chromatin has a wiry, fuzzy appearance. When a cell is getting ready to reproduce itself by splitting into two cells, the chromatin compacts into the form of **chromosomes**.

THE DATA IN THE DNA
DNA Molecules and the Rules of Attraction

DNA molecules and proteins perform very different functions in cells. Yet the two types of molecules share a common feature—they both are **polymers**. A polymer is a large chemical made by combining smaller units. A polymer is like a train. A train is formed by combining smaller cars. Similarly, a protein or a DNA molecule is formed by combining smaller chemicals. In a train, a device called a *coupler* connects the railway cars to each other. In proteins and DNA, small chemicals link with each other by forming a chemical bond. These bonds are created when atoms of two chemicals share electrons. A protein forms when small molecules called **amino acids** connect with each other by chemical bonds.

A DNA molecule is a polymer composed of **nucleotides** linked by chemical bonds. Each nucleotide has three parts: (1) a sugar molecule, (2) a chemical group that contains phosphorus, and (3) a molecule called a **base** that contains nitrogen. The sugar group of one nucleotide binds with the phosphorous group of another nucleotide. A DNA molecule thus has a "sugar-phosphate-sugar-phosphate" structure called the *sugar-phosphate backbone* of DNA.

The bases of nucleotides stick out from the sugar-phosphate backbone. A DNA molecule has four types of bases—adenine (A), cytosine (C), guanine (G), and thymine (T). Scientists refer to the bases by the first letter of their names. For example, "GCATAG" indicates a small piece of DNA that has the base sequence "guanine-cytosine-adenine-thymine-adenine-guanine."

In a chromosome, two molecules of DNA bind to form a double helix. Two DNA strands stay together because certain bases are attracted to each other. This attraction can be imagined as a type of magnetic attraction. The rules of attraction are simple—an A on one strand pairs with a T on the other strand, and a G on one strand pairs with a C on the other strand. When bases of two different DNA strands bind together, they form a **base pair**.

Consider a very short DNA molecule with two strands. One strand has the following sequence: "CATTAGCATGGACT." The other strand would have the sequence "GTAATCGTACCTGA." Together, the strands would appear as follows:

CATTAGCATGGACT

GTAATCGTACCTGA

The strands appear in this manner because the first "C" in CATTAGCATGGACT pairs with the "G" in GTAATCGTACCT-GA, the "A" in CATTAGCATGGACT pairs with the "T" in GTA-

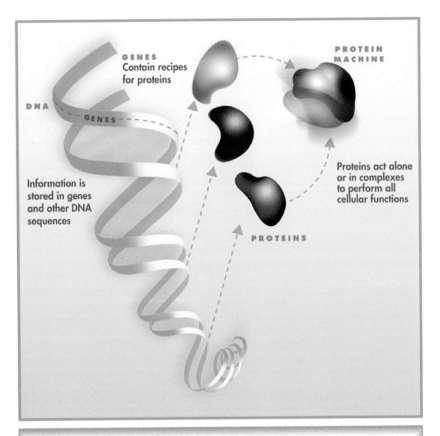

Figure 2.2   Genomes are expressed according to a complex set of directions embedded in the DNA sequence. The products of expression are proteins that do essentially all of the work of the cell: They build cellular structures, digest nutrients, execute other metabolic functions, and mediate much of the information flow within a cell and among cellular communities. To accomplish these tasks, proteins typically work with other proteins or nucleic acids as multicomponent "molecular machines"—structures that fit together and function in highly specific, lock-and-key ways.

ATCGTACCTGA, and so on. Two nucleic acid molecules with nucleotide sequences that allow the molecules to bind with each other by base pairing are said to have **complementary nucleotide sequences**.

A double helix forms because the bases in the strands are attracted to each other. The sequence of bases in either DNA strand does not affect this attraction. However, DNA molecules do not contain bases in a random pattern. In a strand of DNA, the order of bases contains data for assembling proteins.

USE OF THE GENETIC CODE BY CELLS TO DECIPHER INSTRUCTIONS FOR PROTEIN SYNTHESIS

A **gene** is a DNA nucleotide sequence that provides the information that a cell needs to produce a protein. Animals synthesize proteins using about 20 different amino acids. DNA has only four types of nucleotides that instruct the cell to build a protein with 20 types of amino acids. How is this achieved? The instructions of DNA have the form of a code.

Computers also operate by reading a code. Computers read a code based on a series of 0s and 1s. A short string of computer code might appear as follows:

001100111001010101011100101101001

This string of 0s and 1s does not make sense by itself. But computers do not read code simply as a line of 0s and 1s. Instead, a computer divides a series of numbers into segments. Many computers bundle a series of 0s and 1s into groups of eight called *bytes*. Such a computer would read the above series of numbers as the following four distinct units:

00110011 10010101 01011001 01101001

By dividing a series of 0s and 1s into bundles of eight, computer programmers created a code. This code has more than 250 distinct bytes of 0s and 1s. The bytes function as words to provide instructions for the computer.

Nature devised this type of coding system billions of years ago. DNA uses a similar approach in the **genetic code**. Consider the following short nucleotide sequence:

AACCACCCAGAAGGAGCA

Instead of breaking the sequence into bundles of eight like a computer does, the genetic code uses groups of three nucleotides. A group of three nucleotides, called a **codon**, directs a cell to add an amino acid to produce a protein. For example, the above nucleotide sequence is read as follows:

AAC CAC CCA GAA GGA GCA

These codons instruct the protein-making machinery to add amino acids called *asparagine, histidine, proline, glutamic acid, glycine,* and *alanine.*

The Spread of Disease with Climate Changes

In October 2008, health experts from the Wildlife Conservation Society stated that global warming could enable 12 diseases to move into new parts of the world. The diseases could affect the health of humans and wild animals. This was not a wild prediction. The year before, a small village in northern Italy was attacked by a viral disease that did not belong in the region.

Panic spread in the Italian village of Castiglione Di Cervia during August 2007. An increasing number of people became ill with high fever, fatigue, and severe bone pain. Even as the number of affected patients topped 100, doctors could not discover the cause of the mysterious illness. Public officials reported an answer after a month of study. The ill people suffered from a tropical disease called *chikungunya*. The illness, caused by a virus, normally occurs in the Indian Ocean region. Tiger mosquitoes spread the disease by drinking the blood of an infected person. The insects consume viruses with the blood and then pass on the viruses when they bite a healthy person. Tiger mosquitoes have lived in southern Italy for more than 10 years. As Europe becomes warmer, the mosquitoes are moving

THE PRODUCTION OF PROTEINS
Data Transformation within a Cell

The genetic code enables a cell to transform one type of information to another type of information—that is, the code provides the means for a cell to use data stored in DNA's nucleotides to assemble amino acids into proteins. A cell's machinery for producing proteins is usually found outside the nucleus and in the membranes of the endoplasmic reticulum. Because nuclear DNA stays in the nucleus, the cell must have a way to transfer the genetic code data

Figure 2.3   The tiger mosquito is a common carrier of many viruses, including dengue fever, West Nile virus, and yellow fever.

north through northern Italy and into France and Switzerland. This was the first outbreak of a tropical disease in modern Europe.

contained in a DNA molecule to the protein-producing machinery. The transfer of data is performed with molecules of ribonucleic acid (RNA).

An RNA molecule is similar to a DNA molecule, but RNA and DNA differ in three ways. First, RNA has a base called *uracil* that takes the place of thymine in DNA. For example, the "AGA TGT CCT" sequence in a piece of DNA would appear as "AGA UGU CCU" in an RNA molecule. Second, DNA contains *deoxyribose* sugars, whereas RNA contains *ribose* sugars. This is why one is called DNA and the other is called RNA. Third, the structure of RNA differs from that of DNA. RNA usually exists in the form of a single strand, whereas DNA can be found as a double helix.

Messenger RNA (mRNA) is a special type of RNA molecule that transfers DNA's information to the cell's protein-making machinery. Messenger RNA has a nucleotide sequence that is a copy of a nucleotide sequence found in a DNA molecule. Of course, a messenger RNA molecule will not be an exact copy of a DNA molecule's nucleotide sequence because DNA uses thymine, whereas RNA uses uracil. For example, a very small fragment of DNA that encodes a protein might have the nucleotide sequence of "AGA TGT CCT ATA." The copy of this sequence in a messenger RNA molecule would be "AGA UGU CCU AUA."

Here is another way to look at the way that DNA codes for proteins. Consider the following section of a double-stranded DNA molecule that encodes a small protein:

. . . AACCACCTAGAAGGTGCA . . .

. . .TTGGTGGATCTTCCACGT. . .

To transfer genetic code data from the nucleus, a cell synthesizes a messenger RNA molecule from DNA. The process of making an RNA copy of a gene is called **transcription** because the cell transcribes (or copies) DNA. An enzyme called *RNA polymerase* assembles ribonucleotides into an RNA molecule. An enzyme is a protein that increases the rate of a chemical reaction. For this example, suppose that the bottom strand of DNA serves as a template for synthesizing RNA. RNA polymerase travels along this DNA strand, linking ribonucleotides to form RNA. How does RNA polymerase add the correct ribonucleotides? The nucleotide rules of attraction

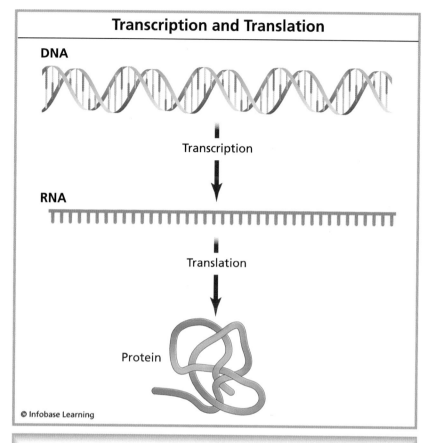

Transcription and Translation

DNA

Transcription

RNA

Translation

Protein

© Infobase Learning

Figure 2.4   In transcription, a complementary RNA copy of a sequence of DNA is made. In translation, the mRNA produced by transcription is decoded by the ribosome to produce a specific amino acid chain that will fold into an active protein.

determine the sequence—that is, U pairs with an A in DNA, A pairs with a T in DNA, and Gs pair with Cs. The new RNA molecule has the following nucleotide sequence:

AACCACCUAGAAGGUGCA

Note that the sequence of the RNA molecule is the RNA version of the nucleotide sequence found in the top strand of the DNA molecule. This strand of DNA is called the *RNA-like strand* or the *sense strand*. The bottom strand of the DNA molecule is called the *template strand* or the **antisense strand**.

PROTEINS AND THEIR SHAPES

After the messenger RNA molecule travels to the cytoplasm, the cell translates the code of the messenger RNA molecule into a string of amino acids that form a protein. The process of making a protein is called **translation**.

Protein synthesis can be imagined as adding amino acid "cars" to a growing protein polymer "train." However, a protein does not have the form of a linear train. Amino acids push and pull a protein into a shape. For example, a protein can have a spiral shape, the shape of a knot, or a combination of these shapes.

Each of the 20 amino acids has two basic components. One part, which is the same in all amino acids, allows amino acids to couple with each other. The other part—a side group—differs among the amino acids. One way to picture a protein is to imagine the identical parts of amino acids forming a chain. Each amino acid has a side group that sticks out from the chain.

The sequence of amino acids determines a protein's shape in the watery environment of a cell. Some side groups are hydrophobic ("water-fearing" groups). These move away from water and toward a protein's dry interior. Hydrophobic groups act like the head of a scared turtle ducking inside the shell. Other side groups are hydrophilic ("water-loving" groups). These side groups move away from the protein's interior to the watery exterior of a protein. Yet other side groups are attracted to each other and bend the protein to move closer together. As amino acid side groups move to new positions, they twist and fold the protein. Their combined activities determine a protein's form. The shape of a protein is critical. A protein's shape determines its function.

A protein may have four types of structure that determine its final shape. The primary structure of a protein is simply the sequence of amino acids in the protein polymer. The secondary structure occurs when a protein's amino acids are linked by weak chemical bonds involving hydrogen atoms. For example, hydrogen bonds can pull one or more sections of a protein chain into a spiral shape. The tertiary structure is formed as amino acid side groups bend, twist, and fold the protein into a complex three-dimensional shape. A protein's tertiary structure is stabilized by chemical bonds between

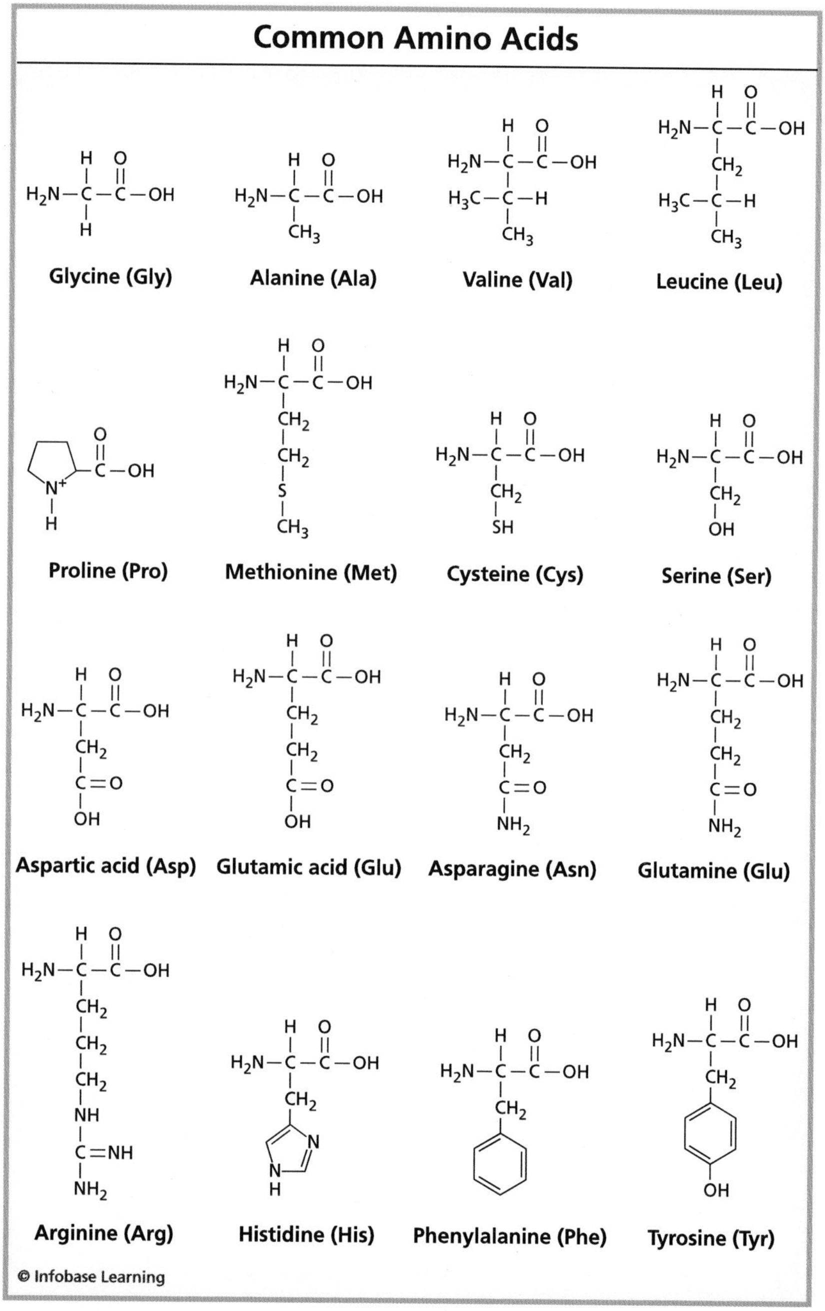

Common Amino Acids

Glycine (Gly)   Alanine (Ala)   Valine (Val)   Leucine (Leu)

Proline (Pro)   Methionine (Met)   Cysteine (Cys)   Serine (Ser)

Aspartic acid (Asp)   Glutamic acid (Glu)   Asparagine (Asn)   Glutamine (Glu)

Arginine (Arg)   Histidine (His)   Phenylalanine (Phe)   Tyrosine (Tyr)

© Infobase Learning

Figure 2.5 The genetic code—the set of rules by which information is encoded in genetic material—is translated in protein, or amino acid sequences. These amino acids are represented in the code.

Deadly Viruses Decide: To Bee or Not To Bee

Since fall 2006, beekeepers in the United States have noticed a decrease in the honey bee population. The decline not only affects the honey supply but also the growth of fruit and vegetable plants that depend upon bees for pollination. Take the apple industry for example. Apple trees depend upon insects for pollination, and honey bees perform 90% of the job.

Although many factors may be responsible for killing bees, one important cause is colony collapse disorder (CCD). When CCD strikes a colony, entire bee populations die, sometimes within several days. In 2007, Diana Cox-Foster, a professor at Pennsylvania State University's College of Agricultural Sciences, reported a link between CCD and the Israeli acute paralysis virus. The virus causes bees to develop shivering wings. In time, the bees become paralyzed and then die. Researchers performed tests in which they infected a healthy honey bee colony with the virus. Within one week, they saw an increase in bee death and the presence of paralytic bees. The scientists suggest that CCD may be caused by the virus in combination with chemicals in the environment, such as pesticides.

A research team at the University of Tokyo reported another type of virus that infects honey bees. This virus makes worker bees hostile. The team named the virus *kakugo*, which means "ready to attack." Worker bees take on different jobs as they grow older. During their first 20 days, young worker bees clean honeycomb cells and feed bee larvae inside the hive. Then they defend the hive against hornets and other predators. Old worker bees forage for pollen and nectar. The scientists found the kakugo virus in the brains of old worker bees that attacked hornets. A virus infection in the brain may freeze worker bees in their guard-duty mode, ready to attack other insects.

pairs of amino acids located in different regions of the protein chain. Some proteins have a quaternary structure in which the active protein molecule contains two or more protein subunits. A protein may have a number of identical subunits or a collection of different subunits.

VIRUSES TAKE CONTROL OF DATA TRANSFORMATION

The process of transcription transforms data in DNA to data in RNA. Translation transforms data in RNA to data in protein. A virus can force a cell to make viral proteins by substituting viral DNA for the cell's DNA or by providing viral RNA for the cell's protein synthesis machinery. Viruses use both tactics for taking over a host cell.

3

The Life Cycle of Viruses

I n their dictionary *Aristotle to Zoos* (Harvard University Press, 1983), Peter and Jane Medawar define a virus as "a piece of bad news wrapped up in protein." The bad news part of the virus is the viral genome in the form of a deoxyribonucleic acid (DNA) or ribonucleic acid (RNA) molecule. The nucleic acid molecule contains instructions that enable a virus to take over a host cell and force the cell to produce proteins and nucleic acid molecules for new viruses. Host cells often become damaged or destroyed in the process.

VIRUS STRUCTURE

Viral Proteins

Outside of a host cell, a virus, sometimes called a *virion*, contains a genome protected by a coating of proteins called a **capsid**. A capsid is a protein shell that has one or two layers. The viral genome is very small and can encode only a small number of proteins. As a result, a capsid may consist of one or a few types of proteins.

An infected host cell produces viral proteins and nucleic acid molecules, which form new viruses. Capsid proteins wrap around a viral nucleic acid molecule to form a structure called the

Virus Structures

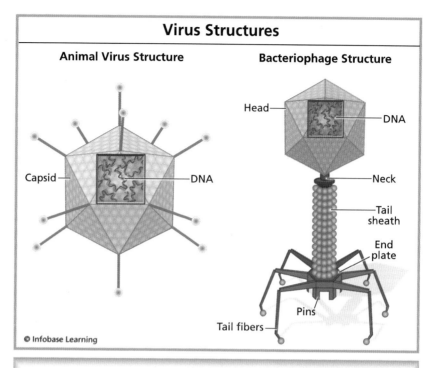

Animal Virus Structure

Bacteriophage Structure

Capsid

DNA

Head

DNA

Neck

Tail sheath

End plate

Pins

Tail fibers

© Infobase Learning

Figure 3.1 Bacterial and animal viruses have different structures. All viruses contain a nucleic acid (RNA or DNA) and a protein coat (capsid) that encases it. The capsid protects the nucleic acid from digestion by enzymes, contains special surface sites to enable it to attach to a host cell, and provides proteins that help the virus particles to penetrate the host cell's membrane.

nucleocapsid. A nucleocapsid is simply a nucleic acid molecule and capsid proteins. The nucleocapsid is very stable and allows viruses to exist in water, air, and the ground.

Capsid proteins wrap around a viral genome in different patterns. For some viruses, capsid proteins and a nucleic acid molecule assemble into a helical structure. These viruses have a capsid with a helical symmetry. Other viruses have capsid proteins and a nucleic acid molecule arranged in an icosahedral symmetry. An icosahedron is a geometric figure with 20 triangular sides. Most capsid proteins are arranged as a helix or in the shape of an icosahedron. Some capsids have the shape of a rod or a cone.

In addition to protecting the nucleic acid molecule, viral proteins enable a virus to invade a host cell. Viral proteins fasten to the membrane of a host cell and help the virus enter the cell. Other viral proteins are needed to make copies of the viral genome. Still other viral proteins interfere with host cell's defense mechanisms, which would otherwise prevent virus production.

VIRAL GENOME

The genome of a virus can be a DNA molecule or an RNA molecule, depending upon the type of virus. The form of the genome also varies. Some viruses have a single-stranded nucleic acid molecule, whereas others have a double-stranded nucleic acid molecule. A virus can have a linear nucleic acid molecule or a circular nucleic acid molecule. A few examples that illustrate the variety of viral genome forms are as follows:

- poxviruses (cause smallpox and other diseases in humans)—linear, double-stranded DNA
- baculoviruses (infect insects)—circular, double-stranded DNA
- tobacco mosaic virus (infects more than 550 plant species)—linear, single-stranded RNA
- hepatitis D virus (causes liver disease in humans)—circular, single-stranded RNA

A virus can contain one of two types of single-stranded RNA molecules. One type of single-stranded RNA can be used by a host cell as a messenger RNA to produce protein. This type of RNA genome is called a *sense strand RNA genome.* The second type of single-stranded RNA genome is called an *antisense RNA genome.* An antisense strand is said to be complementary to a sense strand. Two nucleic acid molecules are complementary to each other if they have nucleotide sequences that allow the molecules to bind with each other by base pairing. For example, the short RNA molecules, GUGCAU and CACGUA, could bind with each other as follows:

GUGCAU

CACGUA

A virus with an antisense RNA genome must coerce a host cell to use the antisense RNA as a template to synthesize a sense RNA strand. The new sense RNA strand can then be used as a messenger RNA to make proteins.

A scientist can ask a number of questions about a viral genome, such as:

- Is the genome a DNA molecule or an RNA molecule?
- Is the genome linear or circular?
- Is the genome a single-stranded molecule or a double-stranded molecule?
- If the genome is a single-stranded RNA molecule, then is the RNA a sense strand or an antisense strand?

The human genome contains 3 billion base pairs. By comparison, viral genomes are very small. Some large viruses have genomes that contain more than one million bases. Other viruses have a genome of less than 2,000 bases. The size of a virus's genome limits the number of proteins that the genome can encode. For example, the tobacco mosaic virus genome encodes only four types of proteins.

VIRAL ENVELOPE

Some viruses consist of a capsid and a genome. Other viruses also have a membrane envelope that covers the nucleocapsid. The envelope contains proteins that help a virus particle enter a host cell. Although many animal viruses have an envelope, enveloped viruses are less common among plant viruses. Enveloped virus particles are very rare among viruses that infect bacteria.

VIRAL REPRODUCTION IN ANIMAL CELLS

Viruses are parasites, but they can be choosy. Some viruses target certain types of cells. For example, the rabies virus infects muscle cells and nerve cells, whereas the rhinovirus infects cells in nasal passages. Some viruses infect cells of certain species. For instance, the poliovirus infects cells of primates. All viruses need a host cell to produce new viruses. Viral genomes are simply too small to

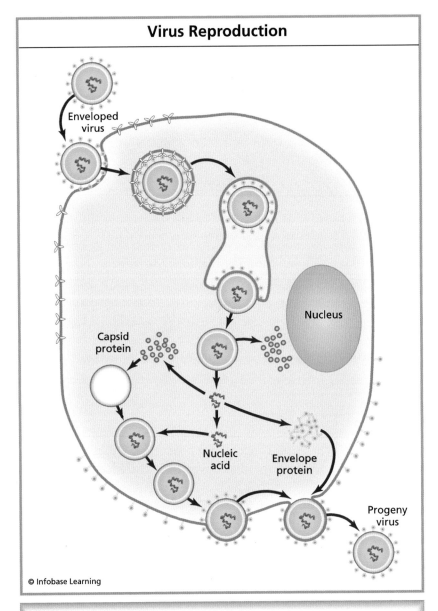

Virus Reproduction

Enveloped virus

Nucleus

Capsid protein

Nucleic acid

Envelope protein

Progeny virus

© Infobase Learning

Figure 3.2 The life cycle of an animal virus includes: absorption by or docking with the host's receptor protein, entry into the host's cytoplasm, biosynthesis of the viral components, assembly of components into complete viral units, and budding from the host cell.

encode the many proteins required for a virus to make copies of itself.

THE STEPS OF VIRAL REPRODUCTION

Before a virus can take over a host cell, it must deliver its genome to the cell's interior. An animal virus begins its invasion by attaching to a host cell. One or more proteins on the surface of the virus bind with receptor proteins on the cell's outer membrane. After binding with receptors, an animal virus crosses the cell membrane and enters the cell. Capsid proteins separate from the viral genome. Free from its protein shell, the nucleic acid molecule is ready to begin reproducing the virus.

An animal virus reproduces mainly in the host cell's cytoplasm or in the host cell's nucleus. The location depends upon the virus and its genome. In general, RNA viruses direct the synthesis of virus molecules and assemble new viruses within the cytoplasm. DNA viruses can direct the synthesis of virus molecules and assemble into new viruses in the nucleus.

After copies of the viral genome and copies of viral proteins assemble, the new viruses are ready to leave. The departure of virus particles can kill a host cell. Typically, naked viruses—viruses that lack an envelope—burst an infected cell when they leave. This violent departure that kills the host cell is called *lysis*. As many as 100,000 virus particles can burst from one host cell.

Most enveloped viruses leave a host cell with less violence. They acquire their envelopes by budding through a host-cell membrane—that is, the viruses push through the elastic cell membrane, stretching the membrane until it pinches off to form the envelope. The budding process may damage the host cell. A small number of enveloped viruses coerce the host cell to make a membrane that forms around the nucleocapsid.

In short, the following steps describe the reproduction of a virus:

1. The virus attaches itself to the host cell.
2. It then invades the host cell.
3. It forces the host cell to make copies of viral nucleic acid molecules and proteins.
4. It assembles viral nucleic acid molecules and proteins into new viruses.
5. The new viruses depart from the host cell.

Once outside the host cell, a virus is inactive. A virus becomes active when it encounters a new host cell. Then, the process of reproduction can begin again.

Infection of a cell does not ensure that the virus can make copies of itself. Viral reproduction can be blocked by a variety of circumstances. Sometimes, reproduction is delayed. In some cases, the viral genome inserts itself into the DNA of the host cell and directs the production of new viruses years later.

A CLOSER LOOK AT DIFFERENCES BETWEEN DNA VIRUSES AND RNA VIRUSES

The many different types of viruses can be grouped by features, such as capsid shape, size, the presence of an envelope around the capsid, or disease caused by the virus. Scientists have used many of these features to classify viruses. Today, viruses are often grouped by the type of viral genome and method used to make copies of the genome. In this classification scheme, viruses are grouped into the following seven classes:

- Viruses with double-stranded DNA genomes
- Viruses with single-stranded DNA genomes
- Viruses with double-stranded RNA genomes
- Viruses with single-stranded sense RNA genomes
- Viruses with single-stranded antisense RNA genomes
- Viruses that make DNA copies of their RNA genomes in a host cell
- Viruses that make RNA copies of their DNA genomes and then make DNA copies of the genome from the RNA copies in a host cell

As the last group shows, viral reproduction can be very complex. Here is a brief look at two tactics for viral genome reproduction.

Class 1 Viruses

This class includes herpes viruses that cause shingles, chickenpox, cold sores, and genital herpes. The genome of double-stranded DNA viruses

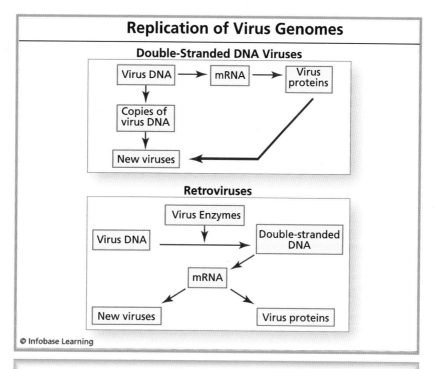

Replication of Virus Genomes

Double-Stranded DNA Viruses

Virus DNA → mRNA → Virus proteins

Virus DNA → Copies of virus DNA → New viruses

Retroviruses

Virus Enzymes

Virus DNA → Double-stranded DNA

mRNA

New viruses · Virus proteins

© Infobase Learning

Figure 3.3   Two types of viruses have very different methods for duplicating their genomes.

travels to the host cell's nucleus. Host-cell enzymes use the viral DNA to produce viral messenger RNAs and copies of viral double-stranded DNA. The cell uses viral messenger RNAs to produce viral proteins.

Class 6 Viruses

These RNA viruses are called **retroviruses**. They include human immunodeficiency virus (HIV), which causes acquired immune deficiency syndrome (AIDS). A retrovirus uses a unique tactic for making copies of itself. Retroviruses produce an enzyme called **reverse transcriptase**. The enzyme uses viral sense RNA to produce single-stranded antisense DNA in the cytoplasm. Single-stranded DNA is used as a template to produce double-stranded DNA, which migrates to the host-cell nucleus. Then, something odd happens. A viral enzyme cuts the DNA of the host cell and seals the

(continues on page 40)

Plant Viruses

Scientists have studied more than 700 types of viruses that infect plants. Many of these viruses damage food crops. Consider the barley yellow dwarf virus. These viruses infect barley, oats, rye, rice, maize, and wheat. Typically, viruses damage plants by killing plant tissues, but they rarely kill a plant host. The damage can be seen as necrosis, an area of dead tissue marked by a dark discoloration. If a plant bears fruit, a virus infection can deform the fruit and reduce yield.

Animal viruses enter a host cell via receptors on the cell surface. Plant cells have sturdy walls that protect them. Most plant viruses infect plant cells with the help of an organism that wounds a plant and that carries a plant virus. The virus infects a new plant host by entering cells through injured cell walls. An organism that carries a virus from an infected host to a healthy host is known as a **vector**. Insects are one type of vector for plant viruses. An insect that carries a plant virus can chew a plant and transfer viruses that enter damaged plant cells.

An outer envelope is a common feature of animal viruses. Most plant viruses lack an envelope. Plant viruses typically have the shape of a helical rod, or they are polyhedron-shaped. Most plant viruses carry their genomes as single-stranded sense RNA. Some plant viruses have genomes in the form of single-stranded antisense RNA, double-stranded RNA, single-stranded DNA, and rarely, double-stranded DNA.

New animal viruses leave their host cells by pushing through the cell membrane or by bursting the cell membrane. Plant viruses have to contend with that tough cell wall. After a virus enters through a breach in the wall, the cell repairs the breach. Plant viruses can leave one host cell to infect neighboring cells by moving through tiny channels called *plasmodesmata*. These channels connect the cytoplasm of neighboring plant cells and allow sugars and

Plant Cell and Plant Virus

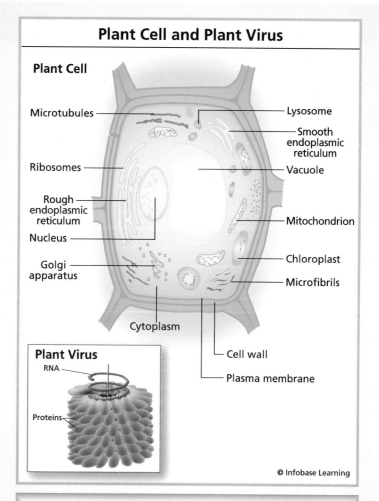

Plant Cell

Microtubules

Ribosomes

Rough endoplasmic reticulum

Nucleus

Golgi apparatus

Cytoplasm

Lysosome

Smooth endoplasmic reticulum

Vacuole

Mitochondrion

Chloroplast

Microfibrils

Cell wall

Plasma membrane

Plant Virus

RNA

Proteins

© Infobase Learning

Figure 3.4 Plant viruses, such as the pictured tobacco mosaic virus, enter a plant cell through a breach in the cell wall.

other small molecules to travel between cells. Plant viruses can cause the channels to open wide enough to allow viruses to travel to the cytoplasm of a neighboring cell. In this way, an infection can spread through a plant and create necrosis. Viruses can also transfer from plant to plant via sap, pollen, and human interference.

(continued from page 37)

double-stranded viral DNA into the opening. The sealed viral DNA is called a *provirus*. When a provirus is active, it serves as a template to produce sense RNA. The cell uses the RNA to make proteins, and the RNA provides the genome for new viruses.

A provirus does not always produce sense RNA immediately after insertion into host-cell DNA. Provirus DNA can quietly reside in host-cell DNA for years before the proviral DNA activates and produces viruses. One reason that a cure has not been developed for HIV infections is that a retrovirus can insert itself into host-cell DNA, which makes the elimination of viral DNA from the body difficult.

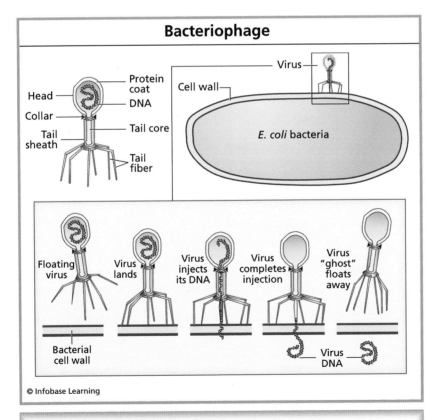

Bacteriophage

Head
Collar
Tail sheath
Protein coat
DNA
Tail core
Tail fiber

Virus
Cell wall
E. coli bacteria

Floating virus
Virus lands
Virus injects its DNA
Virus completes injection
Virus "ghost" floats away

Bacterial cell wall

Virus DNA

© Infobase Learning

Figure 3.5 Bacteriophages settle on the cell wall of a bacterial cell and inject their DNA or RNA into the cell.

THE BACTERIA EATERS

Viruses that attack bacteria, called *bacteriophages*, or *phages*, thrive in the ground and in water. They are the most plentiful microorganisms on the planet. According to Intralytix, Inc., a company that uses phages to develop technology, the total number of phages on Earth is about 100,000,000,000,000,000,000,000,000,000,000. A few drops of fresh water or seawater can contain up to 100 million phages.

Phages have a distinctive shape. Many look like a tiny spider. All phages have a capsid structure called a head. Most phages also have a tail structure, which is a helical, hollow tube. Phages usually have a double-stranded DNA genome. Some phages carry genomes in

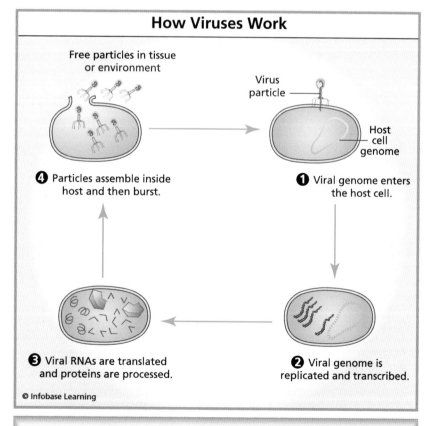

How Viruses Work

Free particles in tissue or environment

Virus particle

Host cell genome

❹ Particles assemble inside host and then burst.

❶ Viral genome enters the host cell.

❸ Viral RNAs are translated and proteins are processed.

❷ Viral genome is replicated and transcribed.

© Infobase Learning

Figure 3.6 Viruses basically trick host cells into becoming "factories" for producing viruses.

Protecting Food with Phages

Bacteria can settle on food products and grow in the food. A person who eats the tainted food may become very ill and even die. The food industry has been plagued by a type of bacteria called *Listeria* that often grows in food production facilities. They can colonize food after the food has been cooked and before it has been packaged. *Listeria* illnesses have one of the highest fatality rates among food borne bacterial diseases. The U.S. Centers for Disease Control and Prevention reports that about 2,500 people become seriously ill with *Listeria* each year in the United States—500 of those infected with the bacteria die. A person who eats food that carries *Listeria* can develop a fever, muscle aches, stomach pains, and other flu-like symptoms. If the bacteria infect the nervous system, they can cause a loss of balance and convulsions.

Outbreaks of *Listeria*-related illnesses have been linked to a variety of tainted foods. *Listeria* bacteria have infected milk, coleslaw, and ready-to-eat meat products, such as hot dogs and deli meats. Refrigerating the food does not help. The bacteria grow on tainted food even after refrigeration. Cooking and reheating can kill *Listeria*; however, many of these food products are meant to be eaten without reheating.

In the war against *Listeria*, the food industry enlisted the aid of phages, a natural killer of the bacteria. In 2006, the United States approved a mixture of six phages as an additive for ready-to-eat foods. Developed by Baltimore-based Intralytix, Inc., the phage mix kills *Listeria* bacteria. Food manufacturers spray the phage mix on food products just before packaging. The phages seek out *Listeria* cells, reproduce, and then kill host cells as they leave. The new phages continue the hunt for bacteria prey.

Intralytix, Inc., is not alone. Companies and research groups around the world are enlisting the aid of tiny phages to improve human health.

the form of single-stranded DNA, single-stranded RNA, or double-stranded RNA.

Unlike animal cells, bacteria have rigid cell walls. After a phage attaches to receptor molecules on the surface of the cell wall, it penetrates the cell wall and inserts its genome into the host cell. The T4 phage is an interesting phage; it looks like a cross between a spider and a syringe. The T4 phage attaches to the bacterial cell wall by its tail fibers. Once anchored to the cell, the tail sheath contracts. This action drives the phage's tail tube through the cell wall. Phage DNA then passes through the tail tube and into the cell. Like an animal virus, a phage uses a host cell to produce copies of itself.

The word *bacteriophage* means bacteria eater. Phages do not actually eat host bacterial cells. In fact, some phages insert their genome into bacterial host-cell DNA and quietly remain there until activated to produce new phages. When it is time for new phages to depart from a host cell, they destroy it. In nature, phages play an important role in regulating the numbers of bacteria.

4

Viruses and Disease

TRANSMISSION OF VIRUSES
The Spread of Viruses by Vectors

A vector is an organism that transmits a virus from an infected host to a healthy plant or animal. Ticks, mites, and insects are typical vectors. Some vectors feed on an infected host. While the vector eats, viruses abandon the host and attach themselves to the vector's mouth parts. Many viruses enter the vector and travel to the salivary glands. In the glands, the viruses are secreted in saliva, ready to move to a new host with the vector's next bite.

Thick cell walls protect plant cells from invasion by viruses. Vectors carry most plant viruses across cell walls. Although aphids are the most common plant vectors, certain fungi also infect plants with viruses. Small animals called *nematodes* are another type of plant vector. Nematodes feed on roots and transmit viruses to root cells.

When mosquitoes feed on the blood of infected animals, they spread many types of viruses to healthy animals. For example, mosquitoes transmit the West Nile virus. Public health officials first detected the virus in the United States in 1999. Since then, the virus has spread across North America. Most people who become infected with the virus experience no symptoms or mild symptoms, such as a skin rash, a fever, or a headache. Sometimes, though, the virus enters the brain, where it can cause nerve tissue to become inflamed.

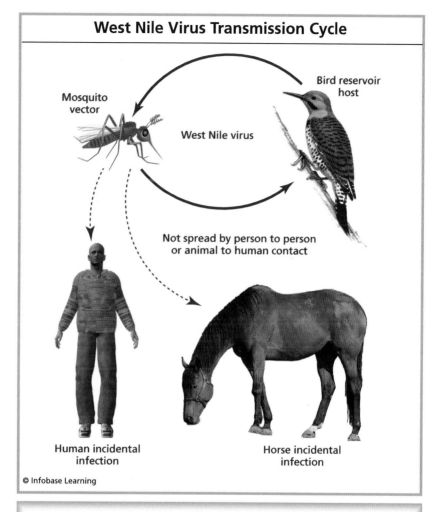

West Nile Virus Transmission Cycle

Mosquito vector

West Nile virus

Bird reservoir host

Not spread by person to person or animal to human contact

Human incidental infection

Horse incidental infection

© Infobase Learning

Figure 4.1 West Nile virus enters the bloodstream of those infected with it. It can only be transmitted by mosquitoes; humans and other animals cannot pass the virus on to other humans or animals.

This inflammation can lead to death. According to the U.S. Centers for Disease Control and Prevention, more than 23,975 people tested positive for a West Nile virus infection between 1999 and 2006, and more than 962 have died from infection.

Wild birds, especially crows and jays, are the main source of West Nile virus in the United States. When a mosquito bites an infected bird, viruses enter the mosquito and eventually settle in its

Triple Threat from a Small Fly

The cucurbit family of crops includes squashes, cucumbers, and melons. Viruses are transmitted to the crops by a fly that looks like a tiny snowflake. In Florida, a silverleaf whitefly infects cucurbit crops with three major viruses. The squash vein yellowing virus kills young watermelon plants. The cucurbit yellow stunting disorder virus causes the leaves in melons, cucumbers, gourds, and squash to turn yellow. The cucurbit leaf crumple virus produces green streaks in yellow squash and destroys their market value. In 2008, scientists at Florida's Agricultural Research Service announced that the whitefly is causing even more trouble for farmers. The whitefly infects green beans with the cucurbit leaf crumple virus. Whiteflies not only damage crops by carrying viruses but also feed on plants.

Farmers have found that whiteflies can resist pesticides. Although the flies may be controlled with more deadly pesticides, the chemicals could pose a threat to the environment. Scientists have been looking at a biological approach using fungi that kill the pesky whiteflies. It may be time to fight flies with fungus.

salivary glands. Viruses move to a new bird host when the infected mosquito bites a healthy bird. The bite allows viruses to enter the new host's bloodstream. Because the West Nile virus mainly infects and reproduces in birds, birds are considered to be **reservoir** hosts. Infected mosquitoes bite other animals and humans, which become incidental or accidental hosts.

Rodents also serve as vectors. In 1993, doctors in the southwestern United States noticed a strange illness. Young adults had flu-like symptoms and experienced difficulty in breathing. Some developed problems with their lungs that caused death. They died from a hantavirus infection. The viruses are carried by the deer mouse, cotton rat, rice rat, and other rodents. Humans acquire the virus by breathing air infected with hantaviruses shed in rodent urine and droppings. Simply sweeping mouse droppings, for example, may be sufficient to stir up tiny particles of virus-infected feces into the air, which can then be inhaled.

VIRUS TRANSMISSION WITHOUT A VECTOR

Viruses do not always need a vector to find a new host. They can use the wind. In 1981, a virus caused a foot-and-mouth disease outbreak in the United Kingdom. The virus had travelled more than 155 miles (250 kilometers) via the air from France to England. Inanimate objects can also become contaminated with virus and spread disease. For instance, contaminated straw and farm vehicles spread foot-and-mouth disease.

Viruses spread among people through various routes, including the following:

* Many viruses infect the mucous membranes of the upper respiratory tract. Sneezing, talking, and coughing propel droplets that contain viruses. Healthy people inhale the droplets, thereby giving the viruses new hosts.
* Viruses that infect the intestinal tract are shed in feces, which can contaminate water and food.
* Viruses in blood can be spread by reusing syringe needles.
* Viruses can spread from an infected mother to her fetus. The rubella virus is one type of virus that can travel from the maternal bloodstream, across the placenta, and into the fetal blood circulation.
* Viruses can find new hosts via sexual contact.

The spread of rhinovirus, which causes the common cold, shows how readily viruses can be transmitted. Usually, colds are passed from person to person by contact, such as a handshake. University of Virginia scientists showed that people infected with rhinovirus leave a coat of germs as they touch common objects. In their study, 15 people suffering from colds stayed in hotel rooms for a day.

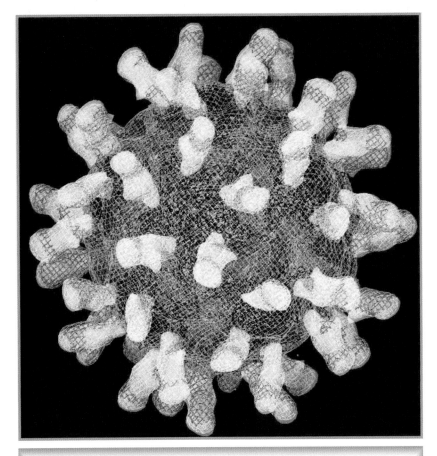

Figure 4.2   This computer-created model shows where the receptors attach to the outer protein shell of the common cold virus. A team of Purdue University researchers, who created this model, has discovered how the virus that causes the common cold infects human cells, a finding that could lead to more effective treatments for the ailment. The common cold virus, rhinovirus 16, contains 60 sites capable of connecting to a receptor, called ICAM-1, on human cells. The virus uses several of these sites to gain entry into the cell.

After they left, researchers tested objects in the room for rhinovirus. About a third of the tested objects contained rhinoviruses, including remote controls, telephones, light switches, pens, faucets, and door handles. After transfer to an object, rhinoviruses remain available to infect a new host for at least one day.

RESISTANCE IS NOT FUTILE

A viral infection transforms an animal's body into a battleground. A contest takes place between the body's defenses and rapidly reproducing viruses. The health of the infected animal is at stake. To win the battle, viruses must overcome the immune system.

The immune system is a group of organs that work together to defend the body against foreign invaders and poisonous substances. Bone marrow, the spleen, tonsils, and other tissues produce and store **white blood cells**. White blood cells are the immune system's soldiers. They hunt, attack, and digest invaders.

White blood cells must distinguish between cells that belong in the body and cells that are foreign to the body. How is this possible? Just as cattle carry the brand of their owner, a body's cells carry identification molecules. These markers can be found on the surface of human cells. A person's immune system attacks a cell that has surface markers unlike those on the body's own cells. The immune system detects the presence of foreign markers on bacteria, viruses, and other harmful invaders.

Shortly after a body is infected with a virus, the nonspecific defenses of its immune system come into play. Nonspecific defenses are part of the **innate immune system**. It is innate in the sense that an animal or person is born with these defenses—in effect, they are "hard-wired" into the body. The defenses are nonspecific in the sense that they simply identify a virus as something foreign to the body. One nonspecific defense is performed by cells called *phagocyte cells* that patrol blood and tissues and eat and digest invaders. Cells called *natural killer cells* identify changes in the surface molecules of virus-infected cells. After recognizing a target cell, natural killer cells bind to them and slay them. These nonspecific immune defenses are considered to be part of the innate immune system.

In addition to nonspecific defenses, an immune system can adapt its defenses to target a particular invading virus. The defenses of the **adaptive immune system** target molecules called **antigens** that are carried by the virus. Certain white blood cells react to a viral antigen by making antibodies. An **antibody** is a protein that binds to an antigen. Virus-specific antibodies bind with viruses and prevent them from entering healthy host cells. Antibodies bind with viral antigens on the surface of infected cells, thus marking the cells for destruction. The body also produces new killer white blood cells that target antigens on the surface of virus-infected cells. These killer cells can destroy target cells by inserting proteins called *perforins* into cell membranes. Perforins form pores in the cell membrane, punching holes that allow the entry of toxins.

A nonspecific response defends the body shortly after it is infected with a virus. The immune system needs more time to mount an effective specific response. An adaptive immune response can take days to weeks to resist a viral infection.

VIRAL INFECTIONS IN ANIMALS

After viruses invade an animal body, an infection follows a certain pattern. Three common disease patterns are acute, chronic, and latent.

Acute infection: The most common pattern is the acute infection in which viruses take over cells, reproduce, and destroy the host cells. Acute infections create chances for the adaptive immune system to limit the infection. The immune system targets viral antigens present on viruses as they travel to new host cells. Viral antigens can appear in the cell membrane of infected cells. The immune system targets these viral antigens and destroys the infected host cell, sometimes before the hijacked cell has completed its manufacture of new viruses.

Chronic infection: In a chronic infection, cells survive an invasion of a virus. Infected host cells continuously produce new viruses. The immune system can target viral antigens on new viruses and on infected host cells.

Latent infection: Some viruses hide from the immune system by infecting a cell without damaging the host cell or by forcing the host cell to make new viruses. The virus genome inserts into the cell genome, or it remains in the host cell as many copies of circular deoxyribonucleic acid (DNA). When a cell divides to produce new cells, the virus DNA is duplicated. The new cells get their copies of viral DNA. Months to years after infection, the virus can activate. Many factors can trigger a latent virus, such as exposure to ultraviolet light or an impairment of the immune system. Once activated, the virus forces the host cell to produce viruses and causes disease in the animal.

Examples of Viral Infections

The most common viral infections are upper respiratory infections. These infections affect the throat, nose, and airways. Infants and the elderly are more likely to experience severe symptoms of respiratory infections. The common cold is one example of an upper respiratory infection. Although many viruses cause colds, rhinoviruses are often the culprit. Contrary to popular belief, a person does not catch a cold by becoming chilled. A healthy person usually gets an infection by contacting the nasal secretions of an infected person and then touching his or her mouth, eyes, or nose. The first symptom appears one to three days after infection—a scratchy or sore throat. As the infection progresses, symptoms include sneezing, a runny nose, coughing, and a general ill feeling. Cold symptoms usually subside in 4 to 14 days.

Influenza viruses also infect the respiratory system, but they travel deeper into the respiratory tract than cold viruses do. Flu viruses also cause more severe symptoms, including fever, headache, and muscle aches. Like a cold, the first symptom of flu—usually a chill—is felt one to four days after infection. This is followed by a fever and pains throughout the body. The most common complication of the flu is pneumonia, an inflammation of one or both lungs. Most symptoms vanish after two or three days. However, fatigue and a cough may persist for weeks. Influenza virus is spread by inhaling virus-bearing droplets sneezed or coughed by an infected person. The droplets can contain 100,000 to 1,000,000 viruses. A person can also get the flu by contacting the nasal secretions of a flu victim and by touching his or her mouth or nose before washing his or her hands.

According to the U.S. Centers for Disease Control and Prevention (CDC), more than 200,000 people each year in the United States are hospitalized from complications from the flu, and about 36,000 people die from the illness. Around the world, influenza breaks out during late fall or early winter. Flu **epidemics** occur when a large number people become sick at the same time in a certain area. Flu

pandemics—worldwide epidemics—have resulted in high numbers of illness and death. Famous flu pandemics include the 1918 Spanish flu, the 1957 Asian flu, the 1968 Hong Kong flu, and the 1977 swine flu.

An infection called *shingles* is caused by the activation of a virus that causes chickenpox. Chickenpox begins when the body is infected by the varicella zoster virus. During the course of the disease, the virus travels in the bloodstream and infects nerve cells. The virus can remain in the latent state in the nerve cells for years and may never become active again. If the virus is activated, it travels along nerve fibers to the skin, causing pain, itching, or tingling. The skin erupts with clusters of painful blisters above infected nerve

Frozen Clues
about the 1918 Spanish Flu

On September 7, 1918, a doctor examined a soldier who had a high fever. This examination took place during World War I at an army training camp near Boston, Massachusetts. The next day, 12 more soldiers reported that they had serious breathing problems. By September 16, 1918, army doctors had 36 additional sick soldiers. Within one week, doctors tried to treat more than 12,000 soldiers in a camp of 45,000. About 15,000 soldiers became sick, and about 800 died.

The disease became known as the Spanish flu. It engulfed the world. The pandemic killed about 20 to 50 million people, including 675,000 in the United States. The disease was unique, because it killed otherwise healthy adults 20 to 40 years old, as well as children and the elderly. Typically, a flu proves lethal only among the very young, the very old, and people who have chronically bad health.

To understand the virus's unique features, scientists began a hunt for the virus in 1995. They found parts of the flu virus's ribonucleic acid (RNA) genome in autopsy fibers. About five days after the blisters appear, they dry and form scabs. The rash normally clears within two to four weeks. Shingles cannot be passed to another person. However, the virus can be spread by direct contact with rash blisters. A healthy person who is exposed to the virus and who has never had chickenpox will develop chickenpox.

VIRUSES CAN CAUSE CANCER

Animal cells reproduce themselves by a method called **mitosis**. One cell divides into two cells called *daughter cells*. The nucleus of

samples taken from two soldiers who had died in 1918. One soldier had been stationed at Fort Jackson, South Carolina, and the other soldier at Camp Upton, New York. The researchers still did not have enough genetic material to study the entire virus genome.

Then, Johan Hultin, a graduate student at the University of Iowa, came to the rescue in 1951 when he traveled with a group of scientists to Alaska to find the 1918 virus. Hultin knew that the 1918 Spanish flu had spread through an Inuit fishing village called Teller Mission (now called Brevig Mission) and 72 flu victims had been buried in permafrost. The 1951 science team wanted to recover flu virus from the lung tissue of the victims, but they failed. In 1997, Johan Hultin returned to the area. He obtained permission from the local council to take frozen lung tissue from four flu victims. Scientists used the tissue to isolate a complete copy of the viral genome.

An investigation of the 1918 flu virus's genes should provide clues about the origin of the virus. The studies may also reveal why the 1918 flu had been so deadly. These insights may help to protect people from another deadly flu outbreak in the future.

Cell Cycle

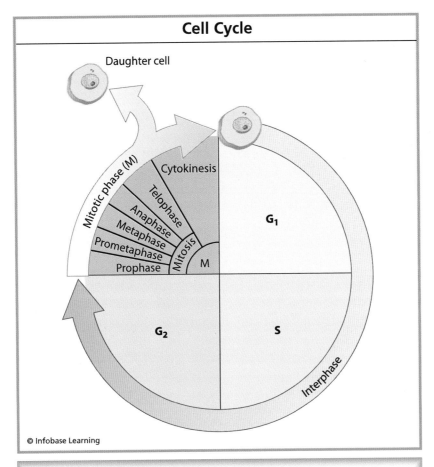

Daughter cell

Figure 4.3 The cell division cycle is a series of events that typically take place in the life of a cell, leading to division and replication.

each daughter cell carries the same genetic information held by the nucleus of the original parent cell. During mitosis, a cell prepares to divide by duplicating its storehouse of DNA. Long molecules of DNA compress into chromosomes. The membrane that surrounds the nucleus breaks down. Like the strands of a spider's web, protein strings shoot out from two sides of the cell and attach to chromosomes. The protein strands pull chromosomes to different sides of the cell so that each side has a copy of the cell's DNA. The cell membrane stretches into the middle of the cell, pinching it into two spheres. When the cell membrane meets itself in the middle of the cell, it splits the old cell into two cells. A membrane forms around the nucleus in each cell to hold the cell's genome.

A cell that is starting to divide enters a part of the cell cycle called the *G1 phase*. During the G1 phase, the cell grows until it reaches a certain size. Then, the cell enters the S phase of DNA synthesis and chromosome duplication. The cell prepares for division during the G2 phase and then enters the mitosis (M) phase. The cell divides to produce two daughter cells.

Many animal cells divide slowly or not at all. Sometimes a normal cell transforms into a tumor cell, which produces daughter cells that constantly divide. Uncontrolled cell division leads to cancer. Various factors trigger the transformation of a normal cell into a tumor cell, including viruses. Viruses that play a role in human cancer are called *tumor viruses*. Most cancers caused by tumor viruses develop after a long period of a chronic viral infection. Viral proteins or viral genes can drive a cell to divide without control. Tumor virus infections alone do not cause cancer. Other factors are involved such as exposure to a chemical in the environment and a deficiency in the immune system. Two examples of tumor viruses are the human papillomavirus and the hepatitis B virus.

Human Papillomavirus

Papillomaviruses are small viruses that carry their genomes as double-stranded DNA. The virus enters the body through abrasions in the skin. Because the virus needs the host-cell machinery to make copies of its DNA, it forces the host cell into the S phase of the cell cycle. The cell undergoes cycles of cell division. Usually, the immune system can defeat the infection. In a small number of people, however, this does not happen. As the infection lingers, cell division continues unchecked, creating a risk of cancer formation. Scientists think that human papillomavirus causes most—if not all—cervical cancer, the third most common cancer in women. The National Cancer Institute estimates that, in 2010, around 12,200 women were diagnosed with cervical cancer in the United States, and 4,210 died of the disease.

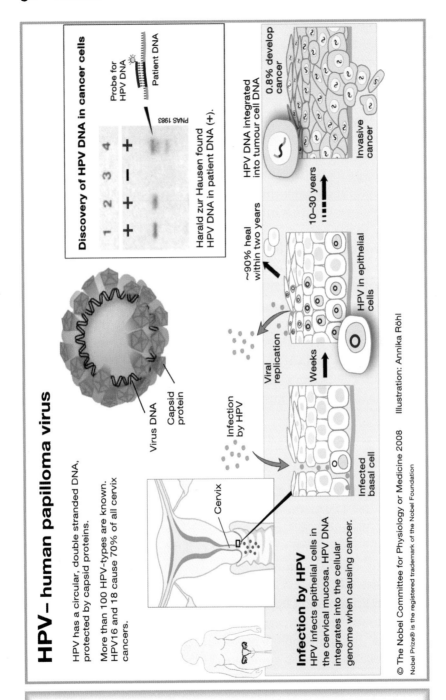

Figure 4.4 Human papillomavirus infects cells in the cervix.

Hepatitis B Virus

Hepatitis is an inflammation of the liver that impairs function. A person can develop hepatitis by ingestion of certain drugs or mold toxins or by alcohol abuse. Viral infection can also produce the disease. In the United States, hepatitis B is one of the most common types of virus that cause hepatitis. A hepatitis B infection can take the form of a mild illness that lasts a few weeks, or an infection can cause a serious, lifelong illness. According to the CDC, 15% to 25% of people with chronic hepatitis B develop serious liver conditions, such as a scarring of the liver or liver cancer. Like the papillomavirus, the hepatitis B virus contains a double-stranded DNA genome.

Not all tumor viruses have DNA genomes. A large number of the viruses that cause animal tumors are retroviruses that carry RNA genomes.

5

Diagnosis of
a Viral Disease

Viruses cause most infectious diseases. The most frequently occurring viral infections are respiratory infections, which affect the throat, nose, and airways. The common cold and influenza are among the most common respiratory infections. Other viruses damage skin, nerves, the liver, the brain, and other organs.

To effectively treat a viral disease, doctors need accurate and quick methods of diagnosis. A patient's symptoms can provide important clues, but a doctor may not be able to make a diagnosis based on that information alone. Consider the flu, for example. At the start of a flu season, doctors occasionally see patients who complain about symptoms typical of the flu. Because many other respiratory infections cause similar symptoms, a doctor needs more data, such as results from laboratory tests, to make a diagnosis.

Three tactics are used to diagnose a viral disease: indirect techniques, serological tests, and direct methods. Indirect methods detect a virus by looking for typical changes that a virus can cause in living cells. Serological techniques look for changes in virus-specific antibodies that circulate in a patient's bloodstream. Both of these approaches ask the same question: Do we see the effects expected if a virus were present? Direct methods tackle diagnosis directly and analyze viral proteins and viral deoxyribonucleic acid (DNA) or ribonucleic acid (RNA).

INDIRECT METHODS FOR DETECTING VIRUSES

Viruses in a patient sample can be detected by injecting a part of the sample into laboratory animals or chicken eggs that have embryos or by adding the sample to cells grown in the laboratory. Typically, cell cultures are used to detect viruses. Most of the cells used for cell culture are obtained from cell lines derived from humans or other animals. As one example, HeLa cells are a line of human cells that scientists have grown in the lab since the early 1950s. HeLa cells can grow side by side as a single layer of cells on the bottom of a plastic or glass dish. This type of single layer culture is called a *monolayer culture*. The cells are covered with liquid containing nutrients that allow the cells to survive and multiply.

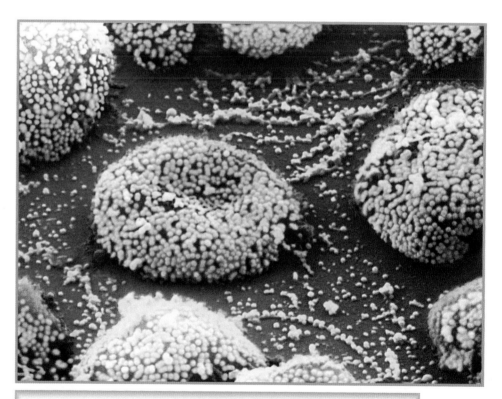

Figure 5.1 The pale specs on red blood cells in this scanning electron microscope image are influenza virus particles.

Many viruses cause predictable changes in infected host cells. The effects of an infection include shrinkage of cells, rounding of cells, and cell death. These changes in host cells are called *cytopathic effects*. *Cytopathic* means that the effects relate to damage in cells. To detect the presence of viruses in a patient, a laboratory technician adds a portion of a patient specimen to cultured cells and then monitors the cells for cytopathic effects. Cultured cells are not only used to detect the presence of viruses in a patient sample, but also to determine the number of viruses in a sample.

Cell cultures offer the easiest way to detect a viral infection. However, the method has drawbacks. Not all types of viruses cause cytopathic effects in cultured cells. Special care is required in storing patient samples because the method only works with live viruses. An infected cell culture poses risks to laboratory personnel. In

HeLa Cells

In February 1951, Howard Jones, a doctor at The Johns Hopkins Hospital in Baltimore, Maryland, examined Henrietta Lacks. He found a tumor on her cervix. The doctor removed a piece of the tumor and sent it to a laboratory for analysis. About a week later, Mrs. Lacks, her husband, and their five children returned to the hospital. The tumor was malignant and had to be treated with radiation. Mrs. Lacks's treatments failed to stop the spread of her tumor. She died in October 1951. Yet a part of her lived on.

Before doctors started radiation treatment, Dr. George Gey was allowed to remove another small section of the tumor. Gey was the head of tissue culture research at Johns Hopkins. For 20 years, he had tried to produce a line of cultured human cells that could be used to study new therapies for cancer. Gey found that Mrs. Lacks's cells were unlike any human cells that he had tried to grow in culture. The cells thrived in tissue culture and produced more cells. Gey named the new cell line HeLa cells in honor of Henrietta Lacks.

addition, traditional methods can require four or five days and up to two weeks for a result, depending upon the virus.

SEROLOGICAL METHODS FOR DETECTING VIRUSES

A patient's immune system reacts to an invading virus by producing antibodies. The bulk of the work carried out by a routine diagnostic virus laboratory focuses on the serological testing of patient blood samples for virus-specific antibodies. The tests identify the presence of viruses difficult to grow in cell cultures. For instance, serological tests are used to diagnose hepatitis B, which cannot be routinely grown in a cell culture.

Gey discovered that the cells were very hardy; HeLa cell cultures can survive shipment in the mail. He mailed cell cultures to associates across the country. The scientists grew the cells and then sent samples to their colleagues. Soon, HeLa cell cultures were traveling around the world.

The availability of HeLa cells became crucial in the struggle against polio. Gey and his colleagues found that polio viruses reproduced in HeLa cells and killed the cells. HeLa cell cultures provided a test for the virus. The Tuskegee Institute in Alabama grew more HeLa cells. Within two years, the institute shipped about 600,000 HeLa cell cultures. Experiments with HeLa cells led to the development of methods for preventing polio infection.

Scientists across the globe continue to grow HeLa cell cultures to study genetics, viral infections, cancer, acquired immune deficiency syndrome, possible drug treatments, and many other pursuits. HeLa cells have even rocketed into space. Scientists aboard an American space shuttle and the Russian Mir space station studied the effects of radiation on the tough cells.

Serological tests also identify virus strains. A virus's genetic material can undergo a **mutation**, which is a change in the genome's nucleotide sequence. Mutations create strains of viruses. If a mutation occurs within a gene, then the viral genome may encode a mutated protein. Antibodies that bind with the viral protein may be used to distinguish between a mutated protein and a protein that does not have a mutated amino acid sequence.

A laboratory can run many types of serological tests. One type of test is called the *enzyme-linked immunosorbent assay* (ELISA). An ELISA can be performed by attaching purified viral antigens to the inside bottom of a plastic dish. A sample obtained from a patient's blood is added to the dish. If a sample contains antibodies that were created for this specific for the viral antigen, the antibodies will bind to the antigen. After washing any unbound antibodies, a second antibody

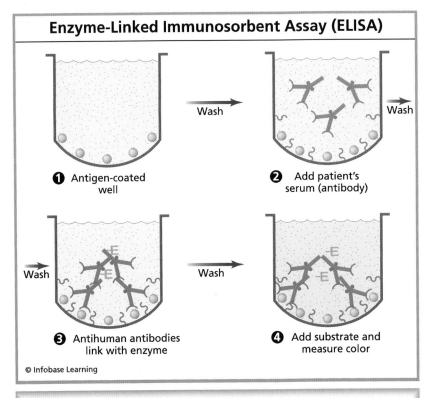

Enzyme-Linked Immunosorbent Assay (ELISA)

Wash

Wash

❶ Antigen-coated well

❷ Add patient's serum (antibody)

Wash

Wash

❸ Antihuman antibodies link with enzyme

❹ Add substrate and measure color

© Infobase Learning

Figure 5.2 ELISA is a biochemical technique used to detect the presence of an antibody or antigen in a sample.

is added to the dish. The second antibody is a purified antibody that binds with human antibodies. These antihuman antibodies have been linked with an enzyme. Unbound antihuman antibodies are washed away. If the patient sample contained antibodies that bind with the viral antigen, then the antigen and two types of antibodies form the following structure:

(dish)—viral antigen—patient antibody—antihuman antibody-enzyme

Next, a chemical substrate for the enzyme is added to the mix. The enzyme alters the substrate from a colorless chemical to a chemical that produces a color. A color change indicates that the second antibody bound with the patient's antibodies, which in turn bound with viral antigens attached to the plate. The results show that the patient's blood contains antibodies that bind with the viral antigen.

Like cell-culture methods, serological testing has its own drawback. Serological tests rely upon the immune system to produce virus-specific antibodies. Specific antibodies often appear in the bloodstream several weeks after a virus infection.

DIRECT METHODS FOR DETECTING VIRUSES

The third approach for detecting viruses is to examine a patient specimen for the presence of viral antigens and viral DNA or RNA. Direct tests often provide results in a short period of time, which may be important for the proper treatment of the patient. Viral antigens can be detected using antibodies. For instance, ELISAs are used to detect hepatitis B proteins in a blood sample. In these tests, purified antibodies that bind with a hepatitis B protein are coated on the interior of a plastic dish. The patient sample is then added to the dish, and the dish is washed to remove any unbound proteins. If the patient sample contains hepatitis B proteins, then the proteins remain bound to the antibodies. A second type of antibody is added to the dish. These antibodies bind with hepatitis B proteins, and they are linked to an enzyme. Because of the presence of the patient's hepatitis B proteins, an "antibody sandwich" forms the following structure:

(dish)—first antibody—hepatitis B protein—second
antibody-enzyme

After washing the dish once again, the enzyme substrate is added. A color change indicates that the second antibodies—and their attached enzyme—bound to hepatitis B proteins from the patient sample.

A mutation in a viral genome may alter a viral protein in a way that prevents purified antibodies from binding with it. If this occurs, an antibody test may falsely indicate that a patient does not have a viral infection. This possible problem with antibodies can be overcome by directly examining viral genomes. Analysis of viral DNA or RNA will also warn a doctor that a patient has a particular mutant of a virus. If so, the doctor may need to modify the patient's treatment.

THE POLYMERASE CHAIN REACTION

A patient sample may contain too few viruses to isolate a sufficient amount of viral genome for analysis. An insufficient number of viruses in a patient sample does not present a problem. Laboratory technicians can increase the amount of viral DNA using the polymerase chain reaction (PCR). If a viral genome has the form of RNA, then RNA can be copied to DNA using purified reverse transcriptase, and then many copies of DNA are produced by PCR.

The PCR process requires heat-resistant DNA polymerase. A DNA polymerase is an enzyme that uses nucleotides to produce DNA. Certain bacteria have DNA polymerases that can resist high temperatures. These bacteria have to make tough enzymes because they live in very hot parts of the world where temperatures run around 212°F (100°C). One type of heat-resistant bacteria lives in a hot spring in Yellowstone National Park.

In the PCR technique, a particular portion of a viral genome is chosen for duplication. The selected portion of the genome is sometimes called the *target nucleotide sequence*. Copies are made with two types of DNA molecules called *primers*. A primer is a single-stranded DNA molecule that has about 20 nucleotides. The primers have nucleotide sequences that allow them to bind with segments of DNA found at both ends of the target nucleotide sequence.

To perform PCR, a technician heats a sample of DNA to separate the strands of double-stranded DNA molecules. The technician cools the sample and adds the two types of primers. Each primer binds to a DNA molecule strand at one end of the target nucleotide sequence. Then, DNA polymerase synthesizes DNA by adding nucleotides to the primers.

While copying DNA, DNA polymerase adds the correct nucleotides according to the nucleotide rules of attraction—that is, T pairs with an A, and G pairs with a C. An example of how a DNA polymerase can extend a primer by adding nucleotides is shown below. The DNA primer is shown in red, and the new nucleotides are shown in blue.

.... GCATGACAGGCCTAAGCTCG

.... CGTACTGTCCGGATTCGAGCGGACATAGCAATTCG ....

↓

....GCATGACAGGCCTAAGCTCGC

.... CGTACTGTCCGGATTCGAGCGGACATAGCAATTCG ....

↓

.... GCATGACAGGCCTAAGCTCGCC

.... CGTACTGTCCGGATTCGAGCGGACATAGCAATTCG ....

↓

.... GCATGACAGGCCTAAGCTCGCCT

.... CGTACTGTCCGGATTCGAGCGGACATAGCAATTCG ....

After completing DNA synthesis, the DNA sample is heated again to separate DNA strands. Cooling the sample allows primers to bind with single-stranded DNA molecules. Another round of

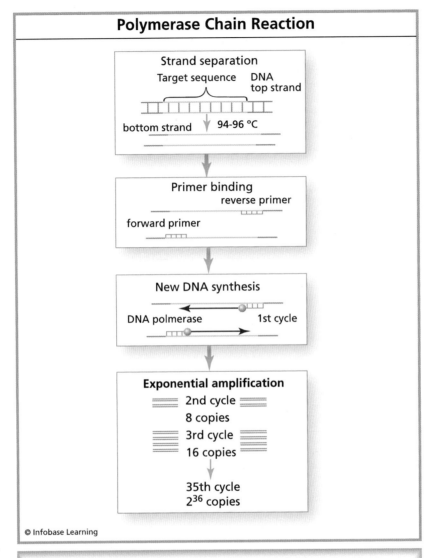

Polymerase Chain Reaction

Strand separation

Target sequence DNA top strand

bottom strand 94-96 °C

Primer binding

reverse primer

forward primer

New DNA synthesis

DNA polmerase 1st cycle

Exponential amplification

2nd cycle
8 copies

3rd cycle
16 copies

35th cycle
2^{36} copies

© Infobase Learning

Figure 5.3 A polymerase chain reaction can generate billions of copies of a particular DNA sequence.

synthesis begins. By repeating these steps, a technician can make one billion copies of the target nucleotide sequence in a few hours.

Detection of a particular virus is shown simply by its ability to make copies of DNA molecules with primers that have a virus-specific nucleotide sequence. A method called *real-time PCR* allows a technician to detect the accumulation of DNA copies as they are synthesized.

RESTRICTION FRAGMENT LENGTH POLYMORPHISM

Depending upon the type of virus that has infected a patient, the specific strain of the virus may determine drugs used for treatment. For example, mutations in hepatitis B virus confer resistance to certain drugs. One approach to searching for a mutation is to make copies of viral genes with PCR and then identify the nucleotide sequences of the genes. To analyze certain viruses, laboratories perform nucleotide sequencing. Another approach for detecting a mutation takes advantage of enzymes produced by bacteria.

Bacteria make proteins called *restriction enzymes*. These enzymes act like small scissors that cut DNA molecules. The enzymes do not cleave DNA at random places. Like a military smart bomb, the enzymes zero in on their targets. A restriction enzyme seeks out a certain nucleotide sequence, which is called a *cleavage site*. A restriction enzyme glides along the backbone of a DNA molecule until it comes across its cleavage site. Then, the enzyme binds to the DNA molecule. Once the enzyme has the DNA backbone in its firm grasp, the enzyme twists into a different shape. As the enzyme contorts, it kinks the DNA molecule and breaks the DNA backbone.

Different restriction enzymes hunt different cleavage sites. For example, a restriction enzyme called *Eco*RI seeks out the nucleotide sequence "GAATTC." In a double-stranded DNA molecule, the cleavage site would appear as follows:

. . .GAATTC. . .

. . .CTTAAG. . .

*Eco*RI breaks a DNA molecule after the guanine (G) nucleotide in the cleavage site.

. . .G   AATTC. . .

. . .CTTAA   G. . .

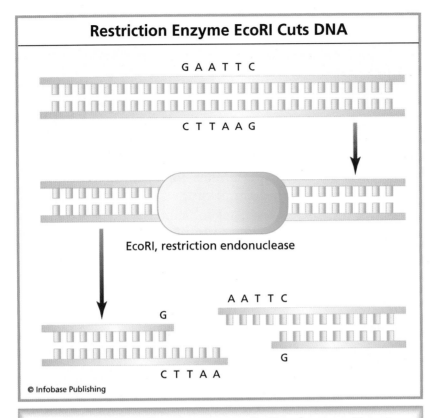

Restriction Enzyme EcoRI Cuts DNA

G A A T T C

C T T A A G

EcoRI, restriction endonuclease

A A T T C

G

G

C T T A A

© Infobase Publishing

Figure 5.4 Tight binding of the enzyme *Eco*RI at the recognition site causes its structure to change, bringing parts of the enzyme necessary for DNA cleavage closer to the DNA strand. Then, the "backbone" of the DNA molecule can be broken to produce two DNA fragments.

Scientists use restriction enzymes to see if a virus is a strain with a certain genetic mutation. This process is possible because a change in nucleotide sequence can create or delete enzyme cleavage sites. One DNA analysis technique that uses restriction enzymes is called *restriction fragment length polymorphism* (RFLP). RFLP is quite a mouthful, but it has a simple meaning. A restriction enzyme cleaves DNA into many fragments of various lengths. *Polymorphism* means that something exists in different forms. A "length polymorphism" is something that exists in different lengths. Therefore, RFLP refers to the ability of restriction enzymes to cleave nonidentical DNA samples into fragments that have different lengths. For virus strains, restriction enzyme digestion produces DNA fragments of different lengths if a mutation in one of the strains eliminated a cleavage site or created a new cleavage site.

A laboratory technician performs the RFLP technique by digesting a DNA sample with a restriction enzyme to produce DNA fragments. DNA fragments are separated by size using electrophoresis, a method in which an electric current separates molecules. Electrophoresis is performed by placing digested DNA samples in a gel slab. An electric current pulls the negatively-charged DNA fragments through the gel and toward the positive electrode at the other end of the gel. The gel acts like a sieve. Smaller DNA fragments tumble through the gel maze faster than large DNA fragments. Electrophoresis separates DNA fragments of different size and creates a pattern of DNA fragments that can look like a bar code.

Here is one example of how RFLP can be used to tell the difference between two strains of a virus. Human T-cell leukemia virus-2 (HTLV-2) is a tumor virus that occurs as Type A and Type B. The RFLP method can distinguish between the two types. HTLV-2 has an RNA genome. Therefore, the first step is to make a DNA copy

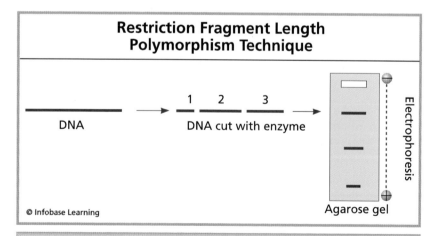

Figure 5.5 RFLP is performed by digesting DNA and separating the fragments by electrophoresis

Virus Traps

Red blood cells are the most common type of cell found in blood. One drop of blood holds millions of red blood cells. The cells appear red, because they are full of hemoglobin protein. Hemoglobin shuttles oxygen from the lungs to tissues and carbon dioxide from the tissues to the lungs. During childhood and through adult life, the bone marrow is the source of new blood cells. Like most cells, a red blood cell develops from a cell that has a nucleus. However, the nucleus shrinks as a cell matures into a red blood cell. In time, a red blood cell ejects its nucleus, possibly to make room for 200 to 300 million hemoglobin molecules.

Nucleus-free red blood cells inspired a fascinating idea. Why not use the cells to trap viruses? A virus that invades a red blood cell cannot control host-cell genes to reproduce itself. The cell chucked out its genes when it discarded its nucleus. More bad news awaits the invading virus. Red blood cells live only a few months before the spleen destroys them. Any viruses trapped inside red blood cells get destroyed as well. Viruses would truly reach a dead end in red blood cell traps.

Coxsackie B virus invades cells of various organs by attaching to a cell membrane protein called *CAR* (coxsackievirus and adenovirus receptor). To test a red blood cell trap for the virus, researchers produced mutant mice with red blood cells that produced CAR in the cell membrane. Then, they infected normal mice and the mutant mice with Coxsackie B virus. Normal mice died within one week of virus infection, whereas the mutant mice lived longer. One-third of the mutant mice survived until the end of the two-week study. At best, the viruses in the mutant mice reproduced at 10% of the levels found in normal mice. The red blood cell virus trap did not work perfectly, but it did show promise. Researchers are developing different types of virus traps to transform a promising idea into a real treatment.

with reverse transcriptase. Then, PCR is used to produce many copies of a section of the viral genome called the *LTR* (long terminal repeat). For both Type A and Type B viruses, the PCR product is a 712 base pair fragment of DNA. PCR alone cannot distinguish between the two types of viruses. RFLP analysis is needed. The identity of a virus type becomes clear after digestion with the restriction enzyme, *Dra*II. Digestion of LTR DNA from Type A virus produces a DNA fragment of 672 base pairs. DNA from Type B virus has an extra *Dra*II cleavage site. As a result, digestion of LTR DNA from Type B virus produces two DNA fragments: one 603 base pair fragment and one 69 base pair fragment. The differences in *Dra*II digestion are easily seen following electrophoresis to separate DNA fragments by size.

Important mutations do not always result in the loss or gain of a cleavage site. Sometimes, it is necessary to make copies of an area of the viral genome by PCR and then perform nucleotide sequence analysis. Nucleotide sequencing is more tedious than RFLP analysis, but sequencing will identify all mutations.

ANOTHER LOOK AT METHODS FOR DIAGNOSIS

Scientists have developed many techniques for detecting viruses and for identifying virus strains. The methods can be grouped according to the question being asked, as follows:

- Does a patient sample contain something that produces effects associated with a virus? This question can be answered with indirect methods that look for cytopathic effects in a cell culture.
- Does a patient's blood contain antibodies that bind specifically with a virus? Serological methods address this question. An ELISA is one example of such a method.
- Does a patient sample contain viral proteins, viral DNA, or viral RNA? This question is answered by direct methods, such as the use of purified antibodies to detect viral protein, or by PCR.

If a test shows that a patient has a viral infection, then a doctor may need to know if the patient has a certain strain of virus. Tests that distinguish among virus strains include RFLP analysis and nucleotide sequencing.

Treatment
of Viral Disease

A common confusion about treating a cold or flu virus infection is that antibiotics can help. Antibiotics are chemicals that treat an infection by bacteria or fungi. They are useless against viruses. In fact, taking an antibiotic for a viral infection can lead to the development of bacteria that resist the antibiotic, and antibiotic-resistant bacteria eventually can cause health problems. Because of this, special drugs had to be developed to fight viral infections.

During the 1960s, scientists thought that viruses used only host-cell enzymes to reproduce. A drug could be designed to interfere with a host-cell enzyme required by a virus, but the drug would also hinder the normal functions of healthy cells. In 1967, Princeton University scientists J.R. Kates and B.R. McAuslan reported that a genome of a virus encodes an enzyme that the virus needs to reproduce itself. The viral enzyme could provide a drug target unique to the invading virus. In time, scientists learned more about viral genes, viral proteins, and virus life cycles. The information guided the development of new antiviral drugs. Although many antiviral treatments require drugs that are small chemicals, some proteins also are used to treat viral infections. The protein drug interferon is an example. One of the latest types of antiviral therapies uses ribonucleic acid (RNA) molecules that destroy viral RNAs.

SYNTHETIC ANTIVIRAL DRUGS

Scientists found most of the early antiviral drugs using massive screening processes. They tested a huge number of chemicals for their ability to inhibit cytopathic effects in virus-infected cell cultures. Over the years, the screening approach has been replaced by methods for designing antiviral drugs.

To design an antiviral drug, a researcher first decides on a step to block in the viral reproduction life cycle. These steps are as follows:

1. The virus attaches to a host cell.
2. The virus enters the host cell.
3. The virus sheds its capsid coat.
4. The virus forces the host cell to make copies of viral nucleic acid molecules and proteins.
5. Viral nucleic acid molecules and proteins assemble into viruses.
6. New viruses depart from the host cell.

After selecting a step to block, a researcher picks a viral protein required for that step and then uses computer programs to design chemicals that should bind to a selected part of the viral protein to inhibit the protein's activity. The analysis requires data about the three-dimensional structure of the viral protein. Scientists obtain protein structure data from techniques such as x-ray crystallography. Just as a beam of visible light scatters, or diffracts, after hitting a glass crystal, an x-ray beam breaks up after hitting a protein that has been crystallized. The scattered x-ray beam forms a diffraction pattern that gives clues about the arrangement of atoms in the protein.

Ideally, an antiviral drug targets a process required for a virus to reproduce itself, but it does not interfere with the function of healthy cells. Finding or designing such a drug has proven difficult. Many antiviral drugs produce toxic side effects in the host organism.

Examples of Antiviral Drugs

Recall that deoxyribonucleic acid (DNA) and RNA molecules are polymers that are composed of nucleotides. Each nucleotide has three parts—a sugar molecule, a chemical group that contains phosphorus, and a base that contains nitrogen. The sugar group of one nucleotide binds with the phosphorous group of another nucleotide. Certain antiviral drugs are nucleotide analogs—that is, the drugs are similar in structure to nucleotides. These drugs hinder synthesis of viral DNA or viral RNA. The addition of an antiviral drug that is a nucleotide analog to a growing nucleic acid molecule ends nucleic acid synthesis. This happens because the nucleotide analog cannot function as a true nucleotide. For example, some analogs lack part of the sugar molecule needed to link the next nucleotide.

Acyclovir is an example of a nucleotide analog used to treat herpes virus infections. The drug inhibits the synthesis of viral DNA, but it has little effect on the synthesis of cell DNA. Azidothymidine (AZT) is an analog used to treat an infection of the human immunodeficiency virus (HIV). An HIV infection damages the immune system. A weak immune system places the body at risk for infections by bacteria, fungi, and various viruses. The condition of impaired immune function caused by an HIV infection is acquired immune deficiency syndrome (AIDS). HIV is a retrovirus. The virus has an RNA genome and produces the reverse transcriptase enzyme to synthesize a strand of DNA from viral RNA. This step is vital for the reproduction of HIV. AZT binds strongly to HIV's reverse transcriptase and inhibits enzyme activity. The enzyme cannot produce DNA copies of the RNA genome.

Another type of drug for treating HIV infection targets a different step of the viral reproduction life cycle. It prevents viruses from entering cells. Remember that some viruses are covered with a membrane. HIV is one of these enveloped viruses. To invade a host cell, the HIV envelope must fuse with the cell membrane. Enfuvirtide and similar anti-HIV drugs prevent fusion and block the entry of the virus.

Some antiviral drugs block the release of new viruses from the infected cell. On the surface of its capsid, the influenza virus has an enzyme called *neuramidase*. As a new flu virus leaves a cell, the enzyme clips a large sugar molecule that tethers the virus to the cell membrane. In 1983, scientists crystallized the flu virus enzyme and learned about its structure. Then they designed "plug drugs." These chemicals bind with neuramidase and plug the part of the enzyme vital for its activity. Oseltamivir is one such drug that doctors use to treat influenza A infections.

Another type of antiflu virus drug was discovered with the screening process. This group of drugs prevents an invading flu virus from shedding its capsid. Trapped within its protein coat, the viral genome cannot take over a host cell and force it to make new flu viruses.

Antiviral drugs slow the spread of an infection and give the immune system time to combat viruses. One type of antiviral treatment called *interferon therapy* is based upon a protein produced by the immune system.

A Coma to Treat Rabies

Rabies is a viral disease often spread through the bite of a rabid mammal, such as an infected raccoon, skunk, or bat. In humans, early symptoms of rabies include headache, fever, and an overall ill feeling. During the next two months, the virus infects the central nervous system and the brain, causing a rabies victim to experience a slight paralysis, agitation, convulsions, difficulty swallowing, and confusion. Once these serious rabies symptoms appear, a rabies victim can die within a week.

To decrease the chance of rabies infection, an animal wound should be thoroughly cleaned. A doctor then treats the bite victim with antibodies and medicine to boost the immune system. Studies suggest that a healthy human immune system can clear a rabies infection if there is sufficient time. However, a rabies infection starts the clock ticking. As the virus infects the brain, it changes brain function. An infected brain can cause death in a number of ways (for example, it can stop the heart or lungs).

In 2004, a 15-year-old girl named Jeanna attended a church service in Fond du Lac, Wisconsin. A bat crashed

THERAPY WITH INTERFERONS

In 1957, Alick Isaacs and Jean Lindenmann of London's National Institute for Medical Research reported their experiments with chick cells infected with flu virus. They found that infected cells secreted a material that interfered with a viral infection of healthy cells. The material not only prevented the infection of healthy cells by flu virus but also blocked infection by other viruses. Further studies showed that the interfering material is a protein. The protein was named *interferon.*

Scientists learned that interferon production is part of an animal's nonspecific immunity defense system. After an infected cell

against an inside window. Jeanna was carefully lifting the animal by its wings to take it outside when the bat twisted and bit a finger on her left hand. She cleaned the tiny bite but did not visit her doctor. About one month later, Jeanna found that her left hand had become numb, her left leg was weak, and she had double vision. She was admitted to a local hospital and then transferred to Children's Hospital of Wisconsin. Doctors took samples of her saliva, skin, blood, and spinal fluid and shipped them to the U.S. Centers for Disease Control and Prevention. The CDC returned a diagnosis of rabies.

By now, the rabies infection was so advanced that normal treatment would not help the girl. The doctors needed a way to stop the virus from sabotaging brain functions so that Jeanna's immune system could fight the virus. They decided to give their patient drugs to put her in a coma. This shut down the parts of the brain that the virus would affect. They also gave her antiviral drugs. A week later, they brought her out of the coma. By then, her immune system was producing large amounts of antibodies to fight the infection. Jeanna survived rabies thanks to a unique therapy.

makes interferon proteins, the cell secretes the interferons. The interferons bind to proteins in the cell membrane of the infected cell and in the cell membranes of nearby cells. Interferon binding sends a signal to a cell that stimulates the synthesis of several defense proteins. One defense protein blocks further protein synthesis, while another defense protein degrades RNA molecules. The activities of the defense proteins prevent the formation of new viruses. They also doom both infected cells and healthy cells.

In effect, interferons defend the body by creating a type of firebreak. Firefighters build a firebreak around a fire to prevent the fire from spreading. To create a firebreak, they clear an area of plants, which removes fuel for a wildfire. Interferons function in a similar way. Interferons cause the death of healthy cells—the source of new viruses—and prevent the spread of a viral infection.

During the late 1970s, scientists invented techniques for producing large amounts of therapeutic proteins in the laboratory. Interferon was one of the first proteins made this way. Since then, doctors have tested many types of interferons for the treatment of viral diseases. Today, interferon therapy is used to treat infections of hepatitis B virus, hepatitis C virus, papillomavirus, herpes zoster, and other viruses.

RNA INTERFERENCE THERAPY

Around 1990, Richard Jorgensen and his team at DNA Plant Technology Corporation in Oakland, California, tried to change the color of petunias by altering gene expression. They produced petunias with cells that had large amounts of chalcone synthase messenger RNA. Chalcone synthase is an enzyme needed for the biosynthesis of pigments responsible for purple coloration. The scientists reasoned that the high levels of enzyme messenger RNA would lead to high levels of enzymes and purple flowers. Yet some plants had white flowers. High levels of chalcone synthase messenger RNA had blocked the synthesis of the purple pigment.

Other researchers reported this strange gene-silencing effect in various plants and animals. One group injected double-stranded RNA into roundworms. The RNA stopped the synthesis of protein encoded by any gene with the same nucleotide sequence as the injected RNA. They named the gene silencing effect **RNA inter-ference**, or RNAi. Scientists now consider RNAi to be a natural process for controlling genes in animal cells, plant cells, and fungal cells.

One type of RNAi process starts with the synthesis of RNA molecules that have nucleotide sequences identical to parts of a gene. An enzyme called *Dicer* cuts the RNA molecules into pieces about 22 nucleotides long. The tiny RNA molecules, called *micro-RNAs*, can inhibit the synthesis of a protein in two ways. In both cases, a micro-RNA binds to a multiple-protein structure called the *RNA-induced silencing complex*, or RISC. When it finds its target messenger RNA, micro-RNA-RISC attaches to the messenger RNA by base-pairing with the micro-RNA. Even though it is bound to micro-RNA-RISC, the messenger RNA binds with the protein synthesis machinery for translation. However, the presence of one or more bulky micro-RNA-RISC bundles clinging to the messenger RNA prevents protein synthesis.

Micro-RNAs also inhibit the production of proteins by destroying messenger RNA before it can reach the protein synthesis machinery. In this route, micro-RNA-RISC attaches to its target messenger RNA by base-pairing; RISC then cleaves the target messenger RNA. As enzymes rapidly degrade the cleaved messenger RNA to bits, micro-RNA-RISC seeks its next messenger RNA target.

Scientists have been developing ways to use RNAi as the basis for treating viral infections. The idea is that RNAi would be designed to target selected viral messenger RNAs for destruction and to shut off the synthesis of proteins encoded by the viral messenger RNAs. One of the companies working on RNAi therapies is Alnylam Pharmaceuticals in Cambridge, Massachusetts. Alnylam Pharmaceuticals scientists produce double-stranded RNA molecules that have a length of about 23 base pairs. These small interfering RNAs (siRNAs) are designed to have nucleotide sequences that match part of the nucleotide sequence in a target messenger RNA molecule. After an siRNA enters a cell, it unwinds and combines with the multiple-protein complex, RISC. When the siRNA-RISC encounters a target messenger RNA, the messenger RNA attaches to the siRNA by base-pairing. This action proves fatal to the messenger RNA, which is cleaved and then degraded. The siRNA-RISC moves on to destroy more target messenger RNAs.

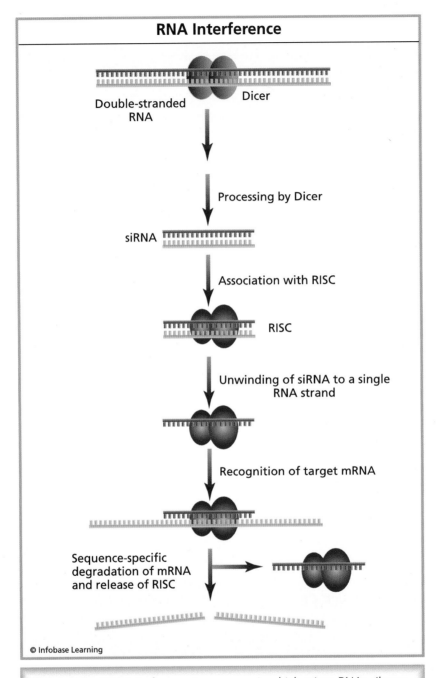

RNA Interference

Double-stranded RNA

Dicer

Processing by Dicer

siRNA

Association with RISC

RISC

Unwinding of siRNA to a single RNA strand

Recognition of target mRNA

Sequence-specific degradation of mRNA and release of RISC

© Infobase Learning

Figure 6.1 RNA interference is a process in which micro-RNAs silence the expression of specific genes.

Alnylam Pharmaceuticals researchers developed an RNAi treatment for respiratory syncytial virus (RSV) infections. RSV is a very contagious virus that infects the lungs. Company scientists designed an siRNA that stops the production of new RSVs. In an infected cell, the siRNA destroys messenger RNA that encodes a viral capsid protein vital for production of new viruses. By destroying

Transforming a Virus into a Treatment

"They will beat their swords into plowshares," states a biblical passage. The idea is to transform weapons of war into objects that have a peaceful use. Scientists are following this idea by converting harmful viruses into new therapies to treat cancer.

Malignant glioma is the most common type of brain tumor. The disease almost always kills the patient. Scientists at Duke University found that glioma cells produce a cell membrane protein called *CD155*. Poliovirus binds with CD155 in the first step of invading a cell. The scientists realized that polioviruses can invade and kill glioma cells. A person who has a glioma cannot be treated with a typical poliovirus because the treatment could produce polio. Therefore, the scientists altered the genes of a poliovirus. The mutant virus cannot cause polio in humans. In laboratory animals, the mutant poliovirus destroyed glioma tumor cells within days.

Scientists at Yonsei University in Seoul, Korea, made a different type of altered virus. This one carries therapeutic molecules inside tumor cells. They tested their virus with human cancer cells grown in culture. The virus transported small interfering RNA molecules that blocked the synthesis of a target protein. The scientists also showed that their virus can carry antitumor drugs to the nucleus of a host cancer cell.

capsid messenger RNA, siRNA stops RSV from invading other lung cells. Alnylam Pharmaceuticals tested the RNAi therapy in human patients during 2008. Scientists at other organizations are developing RNAi therapies to treat infections from many types of viruses, including HIV, hepatitis B virus, hepatitis C virus, and flu virus.

LIMITATIONS OF TREATMENTS FOR VIRAL INFECTIONS

Antiviral therapies can slow the progress of an infection and give the immune system time to clear viruses from the body. The ability of a therapy to hinder an infection comes with a cost—many drugs cause significant toxic side effects. Another tactic in the struggle against viruses is to gear up the adaptive immune system so that it is ready to fight viruses at the first sign of infection. This tactic is the rationale for a **vaccine**, a material that stimulates the immune system.

Prevention of Disease with Vaccines

Politician and inventor Benjamin Franklin once stated, "An ounce of prevention is worth a pound of cure." This notion certainly applies to viral infections. Preventing a viral infection is better than having to cure the infection. Antiviral therapies are not yet available to fight all viral infections. The therapies that do exist often come with their own toxic side effects. Long before the development of antiviral drugs, healers and scientists found a way to protect against viral infections. They used material from an infected person to prevent infection in a healthy person. They essentially fought viruses with viruses.

HELPING THE IMMUNE SYSTEM FIGHT VIRUSES

Smallpox has plagued humans for more than 1,000 years. A smallpox infection covers the body with scarring sores, causes blindness in many, and often kills. During the eighteenth century, smallpox killed one million people in Europe every year. Most of the victims were children. Around 1778, a smallpox epidemic swept through the town of Berkeley in England. A country doctor named Edward

Jenner had no treatment for his smallpox patients. He tried to learn more about the disease and heard a local folk belief that exposure to cowpox might protect against smallpox. Cowpox caused a mild disease in cows and a mild infection in milkmaids who caught the illness from infected cows. It was said that a girl who had avoided a smallpox infection could protect her fair skin by working as a milkmaid. Jenner wondered if he could use cowpox to prevent a person from getting smallpox.

In May 1796, Jenner decided to test the folklore. He used a quill and a lancet to cut two small slits in the arm of eight-year-old James Phipps. Jenner then removed a small amount of fluid from the sores of Sarah Nelmes, a young milkmaid who had cowpox. He dabbed the liquid into the cuts on the boy's arm. About a week later, Phipps complained of mild discomfort that passed within a few days. To test the effect of cowpox exposure, Jenner removed material from the scab of a patient with smallpox and injected it into Phipps. The boy did not become ill with smallpox. Jenner named his method *vaccination*, which comes from a Latin word meaning "pertaining to cows."

In March 1798, smallpox again spread through the area. Jenner vaccinated a number of children, including his 11-month-old son, Robert. The treatment protected the children against smallpox. The practice of cowpox vaccination spread throughout the world. Yet almost a century passed before someone used the idea behind the technique to develop a new vaccine.

During the late nineteenth century, French chemist Louis Pasteur and his colleagues studied the spinal cord of a rabid animal. They found that the agent that caused rabies grew weaker as the infected spinal cords dried in air. To test a possible rabies therapy, they treated dogs with a mixture of air-dried spinal cord. The treated dogs became resistant to a potent strain of the rabies virus even when it was injected directly into the brain. In 1885, Pasteur began to treat humans for rabies infections with injections of air-dried nervous tissue from infected rabbits. This time, doctors and scientists did not forget the idea about fighting viral infections with virus. They soon developed vaccines for other viral infections.

Today, scientists know that a vaccine works by priming the immune system. Recall that the immune system usually responds to invading viruses with nonspecific defenses. Cells of the immune

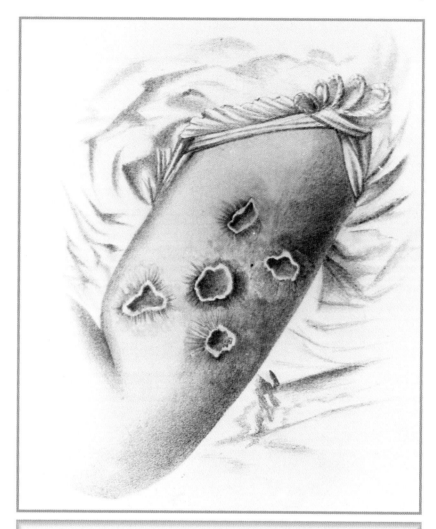

Figure 7.1 This sketch shows the arm of dairymaid Sarah Nelmes, who contracted cowpox.

system seek and destroy viruses because the viruses are identified as something foreign to the body. Days to weeks later, the adaptive immune system initiates a specific response against the viruses. The adaptive immune system targets antigens carried by the viruses. Virus-specific antibodies bind with the antigens and prevent viruses from infecting healthy cells. The immune system's killer cells destroy infected cells that have viral antigens on their cell membranes.

The specific defenses are much more effective in clearing an infection than the nonspecific defenses. But the adaptive immune system has a drawback—it takes time to build a response. An infection may spread and cause a life-threatening illness before the adaptive immune system learns how to fight the virus. This is where vaccination helps. A vaccine exposes the immune system to viral antigens without the danger of a viral infection. The adaptive immune system responds to the viral antigens, making antibodies that bind with the antigens and cells that target viral antigens. The immune system does not forget how to deal with these viral antigens because the immune system produces memory cells. One type of memory cell has virus-specific antibodies in its cell membrane. Memory cells patrol the body until they encounter a virus invader carrying antigens that bind with the cells' antibodies. Then, the memory cells quickly reproduce to create a small army of cells that make antiviral antibodies. Thanks to the vaccine, the invading virus triggers a response from the adaptive immune system days ahead of schedule.

Jenner's cowpox vaccine worked because the cowpox virus and the smallpox virus have similar antigens. When Jenner treated a person with fluid that contained cowpox virus, he provoked an immune response against the antigens. The immune system learned how to take care of the virus. The primed immune system could mount a swift defense against the smallpox virus. The weaker cowpox virus served as a vaccine against the lethal smallpox virus.

TYPES OF VACCINES

The purpose of any virus vaccine is to teach the immune system to create a specific defense against a virus infection. A virus vaccine establishes a memory of viral antigens in the immune system that is triggered if a virus with those antigens invades the body. A successful vaccine may take the following forms:

- live attenuated virus vaccines
- inactivated virus vaccines
- recombinant virus vaccines
- subunit vaccines
- deoxyribonucleic acid (DNA) vaccines

A live attenuated virus vaccine contains a mutated strain of a deadly virus. *Attenuate* means to make something weaker, which is the idea behind this type of vaccine. The mutated strain is weaker than the deadly strain because the mutated virus does not produce disease. However, the mutated virus does reproduce in the body to a limited extent. As a result, the mutant strain produces viral antigens that stimulate the immune system. A vaccine virus must have antigens identical or very similar to those of the deadly virus to allow an immune response against the vaccine virus to protect the body from becoming infected by the deadly strain.

Scientists developed most attenuated virus strains by trial and error. In one method, a deadly virus strain is grown repeatedly in cells that are different from the cells that the virus normally uses as hosts. For example, generations of the yellow fever virus are grown in chicken eggs until mutated viruses no longer produce yellow fever in humans. Live vaccines of attenuated viruses have been developed for measles, polio, mumps, chickenpox, and other diseases.

One risk with a live vaccine is that the virus may mutate as it reproduces and revert to a deadly form of the virus. With this risk in mind, the health agencies of many countries switched from a live polio vaccine to an inactivated polio vaccine.

Inactivated virus vaccines contain killed viruses. The vaccines are made by producing large amounts of the deadly form of a virus and then by treating the viruses to abolish their ability to infect cells. Treating a virus with formaldehyde or another chemical can achieve inactivation. Although the virus is inactivated, its antigens remain intact, and they are able to stimulate a response by the immune system. Killed virus vaccines have been developed for diseases such as polio, hepatitis A, and the flu. Because killed virus vaccines stimulate a weaker immune system response than live virus vaccines do, an individual may require several additional doses to maintain his or her immunity.

Recombinant virus vaccines are the product of genetic engineering. The word *engineering* refers to the use of technology to design and to construct things. Genetic engineering requires the use of technology to isolate, analyze, and modify genes. One of these technologies is **recombinant DNA** technology. Recombinant DNA is DNA that has been altered in the laboratory by the addition or deletion of nucleotide sequences.

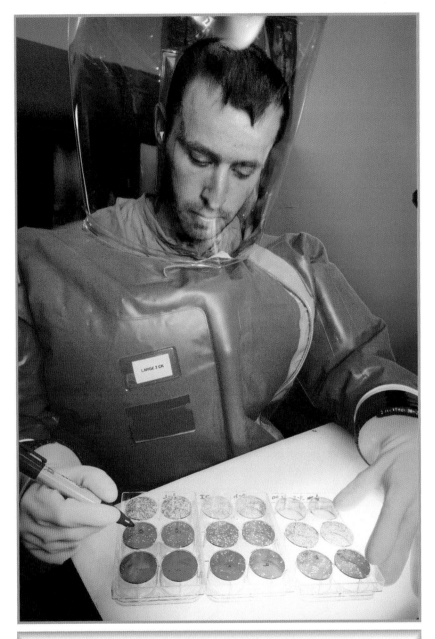

Figure 7.2 Centers for Disease Control microbiologist Zachary Braden is shown counting viral plaques within fixed monolayers of cells, which are set atop a light box. While inside the organization's Biosafety Level 4 laboratory, Braden is outfitted in an orange air-tight suit, which keeps lab researchers free of possible contamination.

The production of a recombinant virus vaccine can begin with a virus that does not cause a disease. A gene encoding a protein from a deadly virus can be inserted into the genome of the harmless virus

Bug Helps Veterinarians with Vaccine Checks

Bluetongue is a viral disease that infects mainly sheep. If an infection spreads throughout a flock, half of the sheep may die. Other animals can be infected with bluetongue, including cattle, goats, buffaloes, camels, and deer. The disease is transmitted by gnats and other biting insects.

One especially deadly strain of the virus appeared in Belgium in 2006. During the next year, the virus spread across northern Europe. To protect their animals, zoo veterinarians decided to use vaccine produced for sheep and cattle. They were faced with a problem: What dosage should they use to vaccinate such widely different animals as camels, giraffes, and other zoo residents? Administering the vaccine posed another difficulty. Animals that roam in large enclosures have to be vaccinated with a dart. Although darts are convenient, they can deliver varying dosages to the animals.

Zoo veterinarians needed a way to check the success of the vaccination. The standard method is to obtain a blood sample and test for antibodies that bind with the bluetongue virus. Certain animals must be sedated before a veterinarian can take blood. Sedation can pose a risk to the animal's health. At the Wuppertal Zoo in Germany, researchers pioneered an unusual way to obtain blood. They enlisted the help of the Mexican kissing bug, a tiny insect that sucks a small amount of blood from an animal. After feeding on a vaccinated animal, the bloated bugs are retrieved by veterinarians who then test the ingested blood for antibodies. Veterinarians at more than a dozen European zoos use the bugs to examine the effectiveness of the bluetongue vaccine.

to make a recombinant virus. For example, a recombinant virus for the vaccination of animals against rabies carries a gene that encodes a rabies viral protein. Florida officials used the vaccine to quell a rabies outbreak. In 1995, rabid raccoons quickly spread rabies to other animals and people in Pinellas County, Florida. The county animal services tempted raccoons with fish meal that contained recombinant rabies vaccine. The program dramatically decreased reported cases of rabies in the area.

Subunit vaccines do not contain viruses; they contain proteins purified from viruses. One subunit vaccine was developed to protect against the flu. Flu viruses carry neuramidase enzymes on the surface of their capsid. The enzyme frees new viruses from an infected cell by cleaving a large sugar molecule that binds the virus to the cell membrane. A subunit flu vaccine contains neuramidase enzymes and stimulates the immune system against the viral protein.

Certain subunit vaccines are produced with recombinant DNA technology. To make a recombinant subunit vaccine for hepatitis B virus, scientists inserted hepatitis B genes into yeast cells. The cells produced hepatitis B proteins that were purified for the vaccine.

A new tactic for vaccination is the use of DNA vaccines. A DNA vaccine is a recombinant DNA molecule that contains a gene for a viral antigen. The DNA is inserted into muscle with a standard injection or into skin cells using a "gene gun" that shoots tiny DNA-coated gold beads. Cells take in the DNA vaccine molecules and produce viral antigens that stimulate the immune system. Experimental DNA vaccines have been developed for the West Nile virus, foot-and-mouth disease virus, and human immunodeficiency virus (HIV).

VACCINE SUCCESSES

Scientists have developed vaccines that prevent diseases caused by more than 15 types of viruses. Successful fights against the poliovirus, smallpox virus, measles virus, and yellow fever virus illustrate the value of vaccines.

Polio

Poliomyelitis, or polio, is a highly infectious viral disease. Poliovirus invades the nervous system and can leave a small number of victims

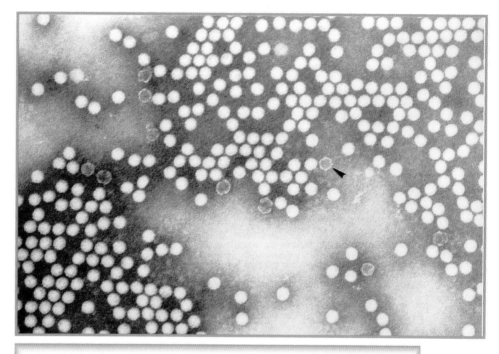

Figure 7.3   This transmission electron micrograph shows poliovirus type 1. Each tiny virus particle is 20 to 30 nanometers in diameter, and has icosahedral symmetry—meaning 20 identical equilateral triangular faces.

with lasting paralysis of the legs and seriously impaired lung function. The paralysis of lung muscles can lead to death.

Polio may date at least to 1500 B.C. Epidemics of polio began to appear in northern Europe in the late 1800s. From then on, people living in moderate climates have experienced seasonal polio outbreaks that peak in the summer months. In 1916, the United States had one of the worst polio epidemics of the twentieth century. The disease killed 6,000 people and left 27,000 paralyzed. Scientists discovered that a filterable agent—a virus—caused polio. In 1949, researchers devised a way to grow poliovirus in cultured cells to enable work on a vaccine.

During the early 1950s, while the United States suffered its most deadly polio epidemic, medical researcher and virologist Jonas Salk finished his polio vaccine. Salk produced the vaccine by growing poliovirus in monkey cell cultures, harvesting viruses, and inactivating the viruses with chemical treatment. The vaccine effectively protected against polio. In 1963, medical researcher Albert Sabin announced his vaccine of attenuated polioviruses. Unlike the Salk vaccine, which has to be injected, the Sabin vaccine is administered as several drops on the tongue. The use of the vaccines brought a decline in polio. In the United States, the last case of polio caused by a typical virus infection was reported in 1979. Vaccination programs promoted by international organizations eradicated poliovirus in the Western Hemisphere by 1990. Public health officials continue to abolish poliovirus from the world.

Smallpox

For thousands of years, humans have endured outbreaks of smallpox. In the twentieth century alone, the disease killed about 300 million people. A person can feel healthy for about two weeks after exposure to the smallpox virus. Then the symptoms of infection appear— weakness, a fever that can reach 101°F to 104°F (about 38°C to 40°C), aches throughout the body, and sometimes vomiting. After several days, small red spots form in the mouth and on the tongue. Within a day, a rash spreads from the face to the arms and legs. Over the next three weeks, the rash turns into fluid-filled bumps. The bumps scab over, and then the scabs fall off. The scabs leave marks that become pitted scars. An infected person can spread the virus when the red spots first appear in the mouth. A smallpox victim remains contagious until the last scab falls off. Smallpox can spread by direct contact with an infected person. The disease can also spread by contact with the bodily fluids of a person who has smallpox or contact with the clothing or other objects contaminated by an infected person.

During the tenth or eleventh century in Central Asia, healers exposed healthy people to low doses of smallpox material to build a resistance to the disease. One method required the collection of dried smallpox scabs. A healer ground the scabs into powder, which would be inhaled by a healthy person. In another method, a healer scratched the arm of a healthy person and rubbed liquid from a smallpox sore into the scratch. The second method became popular in Europe. Edward Jenner used a variation of the technique when he rubbed liquid from a cowpox sore into a number of small pricks through the skin of a healthy patient. Jenner named his technique *vaccination* to distinguish it from the traditional methods that exposed a healthy person to smallpox.

Scientists still have not developed a specific treatment for smallpox. The only way to fight the disease is to prevent it with a vaccine. Vaccination programs and methods to control smallpox outbreaks eliminated the disease from the United States by 1949. Yet smallpox continued to plague tens of millions of people worldwide each year. In 1967, the World Health Organization launched a vaccination program to abolish smallpox, which still threatened 60% of the world's population. It worked. The year 1977 marks the last reported natural case of smallpox. By 1980, the World Health Organization announced worldwide eradication of smallpox.

Measles

Measles is a disease that has existed at least since A.D. 900 when Persian physician ar-Razi wrote a description of typical measles symptoms. Measles is transmitted by infected droplets propelled with a cough, a sneeze, or even while talking. Two to four days after infection, the virus reproduces in cells that line the back of the throat and in lung cells. The virus then spreads throughout the body, causing fever, weakness, loss of appetite, a cough, and a rash.

The measles virus weakens the immune system and makes a person at risk for other infections. The most serious consequences of measles include blindness, an infection of the brain, ear infections, and lung infections. The most common cause of death associated with measles is pneumonia, an inflammation of the lungs.

In 1961, John Enders of Harvard Medical School reported that the measles viral infection can be prevented by vaccination with an attenuated live virus vaccine. One method used to produce the vaccine is to obtain the measles virus from an infected person and to grow the virus in the laboratory using chick embryo cells. As the virus becomes more efficient at reproducing in chick cells, it becomes less efficient at reproducing in human cells. After the live vaccine is given to a human, the virus reproduces slightly before the immune system clears it from the body. The exposure is sufficient to create long-term immunity.

Measles vaccination programs have decreased deaths from measles around the world. Since November 2002, health officials no

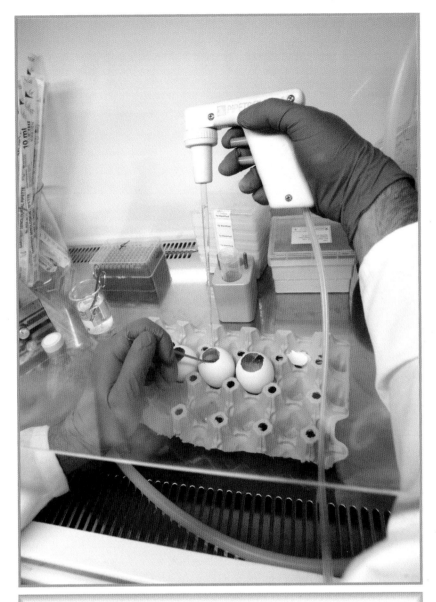

Figure 7.4 A laboratory technician performs virology research on a chicken egg.

longer consider measles to be a common disease in the Americas. International health organizations have called upon countries to drastically reduce global measles deaths through vaccination.

Yellow Fever

In the nineteenth century, yellow fever became one of the most feared diseases in the Americas. Yellow fever causes liver damage and severe bleeding, and it can kill one out of five disease victims. During the Spanish-American War of 1898, yellow fever killed more soldiers than the war itself. After the war, a group headed by U.S. Army surgeon Walter Reed investigated yellow fever in Cuba. Reed and his coworkers showed that a mosquito transmitted the disease to humans. They also provided evidence that a virus causes yellow fever.

At the Rockefeller Foundation in New York City, virologist Max Theiler and his colleagues tried to grow the yellow fever virus in the laboratory. In 1937, they succeeded with chick embryos. By growing generations of the yellow fever virus in chick eggs, they produced

Edible Vaccines

Australian scientist Barry J. Marshall and colleagues used genetic engineering to turn bacteria into a new type of vaccine. *Helicobacter pylori* is a type of bacteria that lives in the stomach lining of about half of the people in the world. Usually, the bacteria do not produce any symptoms. Marshall altered bacteria to carry genes that encode flu viral proteins. The new vaccine works like this: After ingestion, the modified bacteria settle into the stomach where they reproduce and synthesize flu viral proteins. The viral proteins then stimulate the immune system to protect against flu virus.

To test the vaccine, scientists infected mice with the modified bacteria. The bacteria colonized the stomachs of the mice and produced flu viral proteins. In time, the blood of the mice carried antibodies that bind flu viruses. Scientists must perform many tests before the modified bacteria can be given to humans. Still, Marshall predicts that yogurt containing genetically modified bacteria may be available by 2013.

attenuated viruses. When injected into a person, the weak viruses stimulate an immune response that protects against yellow fever. The yellow fever virus vaccine is still produced by cultivating viruses through chicken eggs.

Although a vaccine protects a person against the yellow fever virus, a mass vaccination program will not rid the world of the virus. The yellow fever virus persists in nature as mosquitoes transfer the virus among nonhuman primates. In this way, the yellow fever virus is very different from the poliovirus, smallpox virus, and measles virus, which infect only humans. Therefore, the vaccination of humans can rid the planet of viruses that cause polio, smallpox, and measles.

8

Viral Mutations and Emerging Viruses

Scientists first identified the West Nile virus in Africa more than 70 years ago. The virus normally reproduces in birds, which are the natural reservoir for the West Nile virus. Mosquitoes that bite infected birds spread the virus to healthy birds. Infected mosquitoes also spread the virus to other animals and humans. In the past, the bite of an infected mosquito would cause a mild fever in humans. During the mid-1990s, the West Nile virus became more deadly to humans, inflicting serious brain infections. By the end of the decade, the deadly form of the virus had arrived in North America. According to the U.S. Centers for Disease Control and Prevention (CDC), the agency received reports of about 1,021 cases of human West Nile virus illness in 2010, including 57 deaths.

Why did the virus become so deadly? Scientists examined genes of 21 types of West Nile virus and found a gene mutation that caused a change of a single amino acid. The mutation of the same amino acid had occurred three different times. Each time, the mutated virus was associated with outbreaks of human disease. The amino acid mutation occurs in an enzyme called *helicase*, which the West Nile virus needs to reproduce itself. The mutant helicase enables the virus to multiply at high rates and overwhelm the body's defenses. A helicase mutation can explain why the West Nile virus has become a killer.

Genetic mutations not only make viruses more deadly but can also make them resistant to antiviral drugs. A mutation can also enable a virus to dodge the immune system by altering the shape of viral antigens so that they no longer bind with antibodies.

GENE MUTATIONS

A gene is a deoxyribonucleic acid (DNA) nucleotide sequence that provides the data that a cell needs to produce a protein. Messenger ribonucleic acid (RNA) molecules carry this information from a DNA molecule to the protein synthesis machinery. The genetic code enables a cell to translate the four nucleotides of an RNA molecule into instructions for assembling amino acids into proteins.

The genetic code is based on codons, triplets of the four nucleotide bases found in RNA—adenine (A), guanine (G), cytosine (C), and uracil (U). A coding system based on a series of three of four possible bases yields 64 (4 x 4 x 4) possible combinations. Cells use all 64 codons, and yet, there are only 20 common amino acids. Some amino acids are encoded by two or more codons. For example, the amino acid leucine is encoded by the codons UUA, UUG, CUU, CUA, CUC, and CUG.

Some codons serve as start and stop signals for protein synthesis. The codon AUG encodes the amino acid methionine. AUG also signals the place in the nucleotide sequence of a messenger RNA where the code for a protein begins. By marking the point where the protein encoding sequence starts, the AUG codon determines how the sequence should be grouped into triplets. The AUG codon creates the reading frame for the nucleotide sequence. For example, consider the following the nucleotide sequence:

GCAAGGCCGAUGGGGCGAAUUGCCUGCCCGUGA

The AUG codon creates a reading frame and signals that the nucleotide sequence should be read as follows:

AUG GGG CGA AUU GCC UGC CCG UGA

The genetic code signals the end of protein synthesis with a stop codon. In the example above, a UGA codon signals the end of a

Genetic Code

Second letter

First letter		U	C	A	G	Third letter
U		UUU UUC Phenyl-alanine	UCU UCC UCA UCG Serine	UAU UAC Tyrosine	UGU UGC Cysteine	U C
		UUA UUG Leucine		UAA Stop codon UAG Stop codon	UGA Stop codon	A
					UGG Tryptophan	G
C		CUU CUC CUA CUG Leucine	CCU CCC CCA CCG Proline	CAU CAC Histidine	CGU CGC CGA CGG Arginine	U C
				CAA CAG Glutamine		A G
A		AUU AUC AUA Isoleucine	ACU ACC ACA ACG Threonine	AAU AAC Asparagine	AGU AGC Serine	U C
		AUG Methionine		AAA AAG Lysine	AGA AGG Arginine	A G
G		GUU GUC GUA GUG Valine	GCU GCC GCA GCG Alanine	GAU GAC Aspartic acid	GGU GGC GGA GGG Glycine	U C
				GAA GAG Glutamic acid		A G

Figure 8.1 This table provides a guide to how different combinations of the four nucleotides in RNA encode different amino acids.

protein-encoding nucleotide sequence. UAA and UAG are also stop codons. Sometimes, the stop codons are called *nonsense codons*.

A gene mutation can take many forms. Some mutations are caused by a single base change, whereas others are caused by a large alteration in a gene, the loss of a gene, or the gain of a new gene. The addition or deletion of a single nucleotide can create a frameshift mutation. This type of mutation changes the reading frame of a nucleotide sequence that encodes a protein. By shifting the way that messenger RNA bases are grouped into three, the mutation alters the series of amino acids. Consider the following short piece of messenger RNA that encodes the amino acid sequence leucine-valine-alanine-glutamine:

CUU GUU GCU CAA

Suppose that a mutation in DNA results in the loss of the first uracil in the messenger RNA. The reading frame shifts to the following sequence:

CUG UUG CUC AA

The new sequence encodes leucine-leucine-leucine with two adenine bases left over.

Now, suppose that a mutation caused the addition of a base in the original nucleotide sequence. For example, a guanine is added next to the first guanine in the sequence. The mutated sequence would be grouped as

CUU GGU UGC UCA A

This sequence encodes leucine-glycine-cysteine-serine with an adenine left over.

Single nucleotide mutations not only cause the loss or gain of a nucleotide but can also replace one nucleotide with another. A nucleotide replacement can affect a codon in one of three ways.

In a silent mutation, the mutated codon still encodes the same amino acid. For instance, the mutation of CAA to CAG does not affect the amino acid added to a protein; both codons encode the amino acid glutamine.

In a nonsense mutation, a nucleotide replacement creates a stop codon from a codon that encoded an amino acid. The mutation of CAA to UAA is a nonsense mutation. Because protein synthesis stops early, a nonsense mutation results in a shortened protein. The short protein may not function or may function poorly.

In a missense mutation, the mutation alters a codon for one amino acid to a codon for a different amino acid. For example, the mutation of CAA to GAA would replace glutamine with glutamic acid. A missense mutation can have little effect on protein function or the mutation can greatly alter protein function.

Mutations of single nucleotide additions, deletions, or replacements are common during viral replication. Enzymes that synthesize many copies of viral DNA and RNA molecules make errors. Viruses that have an RNA genome are more likely to acquire mutations because their RNA synthesizing enzymes are unable to proofread and correct errors. Sometimes mutations occur in genes that encode proteins that are targets for antiviral drugs. As a result, a mutated virus can become resistant to drugs. For example, a nucleotide analog drug called *ganciclovir* is used to treat human cytomegalovirus infections. As a nucleotide analog, the drug's function is to block the synthesis of cytomegalovirus DNA. Some cytomegaloviruses have a mutation in the gene that encodes the viral DNA synthesizing

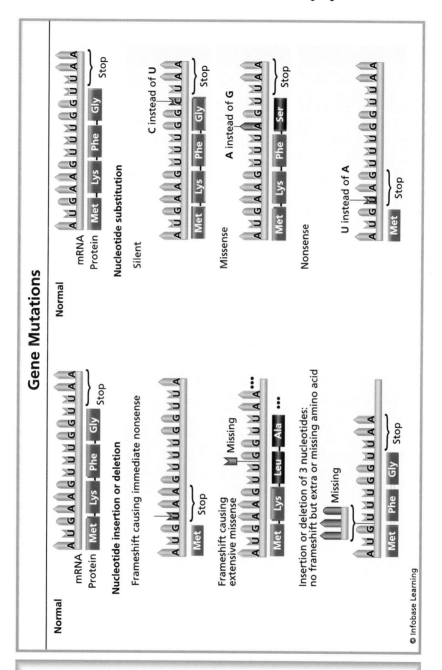

Figure 8.2 Gene mutations can take various forms. For example, a frameshift mutation changes the amino acid sequence of a protein as nucleotides are added or deleted. A silent mutation, on the other hand, will not result in a change to the amino acid sequence.

enzyme. One type of missense mutation causes a replacement of a single amino acid that alters the structure of the enzyme. The antiviral drug binds less efficiently to the mutated enzyme. The treatment of a viral infection with antiviral drugs exerts a selection pressure that favors certain mutations. If a mutation occurs during drug treatment, mutants that resist the drug can continue to reproduce.

Mutations in viruses also pose health problems when they change the shape of viral proteins so that they can no longer bind with antibodies. Mutants of the common flu virus illustrate these types of changes in viral proteins.

INFLUENZA VIRUS AND ITS MUTANTS

The influenza virus has two main forms called *Type A* and *Type B*. Influenza A infects birds and people, whereas influenza B infects only people. Influenza A has caused epidemics and pandemics throughout human history. The flu virus has two proteins called *neuramidase* (N protein) and *hemagglutinin* (H protein) in its capsid. The N protein is an enzyme that plays an important role in the release of new viruses from a host cell. The H protein enables a virus to invade a cell. The viral H protein binds with a protein on the cellular membrane, fitting like a key in a lock. After binding, the virus enters the cell and begins the process of reproducing itself.

Flu epidemics and pandemics result from changes in the H and N proteins that alter protein shape. Antibodies no longer bind with the mutated proteins, and the immune system cannot clear an infection by targeting viral antigens. Genetic mutations that create new virus strains can occur by **antigenic drift** and **antigenic shift**.

Antigenic drift refers to small changes in H and N genes that happen over a period of time. Most of the mutations do not affect the shape of the H and N proteins. However, some mutations do alter protein shapes, and the immune system may not recognize them.

When an antigenic shift occurs, the influenza A virus acquires a new H gene or a new N gene. Many people will be unable to quickly produce antibodies against viruses with the new gene. As a result, an antigenic shift can cause a high number of illnesses and deaths. An antigenic shift can start with the infection of pig lung cells with an influenza A virus that usually infects birds and with an influenza

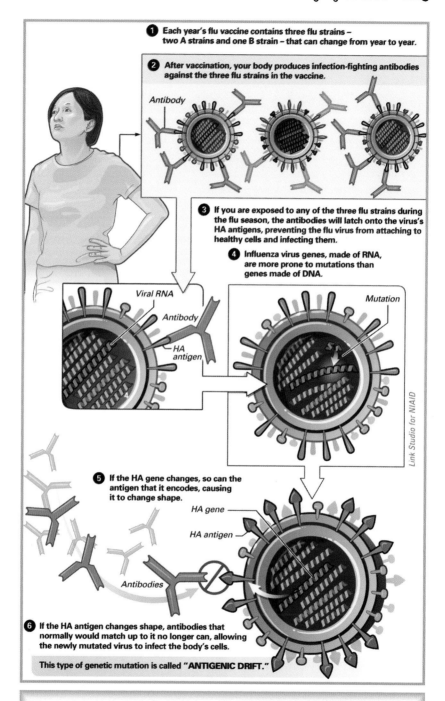

1. Each year's flu vaccine contains three flu strains – two A strains and one B strain – that can change from year to year.

2. After vaccination, your body produces infection-fighting antibodies against the three flu strains in the vaccine.

Antibody

3. If you are exposed to any of the three flu strains during the flu season, the antibodies will latch onto the virus's HA antigens, preventing the flu virus from attaching to healthy cells and infecting them.

4. Influenza virus genes, made of RNA, are more prone to mutations than genes made of DNA.

Viral RNA

Antibody

HA antigen

Mutation

Link Studio for NIAID

5. If the HA gene changes, so can the antigen that it encodes, causing it to change shape.

HA gene

HA antigen

Antibodies

6. If the HA antigen changes shape, antibodies that normally would match up to it no longer can, allowing the newly mutated virus to infect the body's cells.

This type of genetic mutation is called "**ANTIGENIC DRIFT.**"

Figure 8.3   Mutating flu genes create a challenge for producing an effective flu vaccine.

A virus that typically affects only humans. Inside the infected cell, parts of genes or entire genes are swapped between the two virus strains, thus creating a new type of influenza A virus.

H genes and N genes can be swapped to produce many combinations. Scientists have identified 16 types of H protein and 9 types of N protein. Antigenic shifts in influenza A viruses occur about every 10 to 40 years. Since 1900, three flu pandemics and several pandemic threats have been recorded:

- The Spanish flu pandemic of 1918 was caused by the influenza A virus with Type 1 H protein and Type 1 N protein (H1N1). This giant pandemic caused about 20% to 40% of the worldwide population to become sick. More than 50 million people died.
- The Asian flu pandemic of 1957 was caused by an H2N2 flu virus. Scientists quickly identified the virus and produced a vaccine to protect against it.
- The Hong Kong flu pandemic of 1968 was caused by an H3N2 flu virus. Because the Hong Kong flu virus was similar to the Asian flu virus, an earlier infection by the Asian flu virus could have provided some immunity to the Hong Kong virus and reduced the severity of illness.
- The 1977 Russian flu threat was caused by an H1N1 flu virus. Illness occurred mainly in children because many adults had been exposed to the viral antigens.
- The 1997 avian flu threat started in Hong Kong with a bird H5N1 flu virus that caused an outbreak of serious disease in poultry. Six of the 18 people who also became infected died. This flu virus had spread directly from chickens to humans. The virus had not been altered by infecting pigs as an intermediate host. H5N1 viruses appeared in a number of Asian countries in 2003, in Europe in 2005, and in Africa in 2006.

A flu vaccine often has proteins from three virus strains. Every year, at least one of the three virus strains has to be changed to reflect the types of flu viruses that are infecting people at the time. World Health Organization experts review the flu viruses circulating in the Northern and Southern Hemispheres. Based on the data, they recommend vaccine strains to match the recent viral strains to

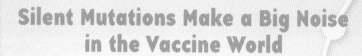

Silent Mutations Make a Big Noise in the Vaccine World

The genetic code has an interesting feature. Many amino acids are encoded by more than one codon. On Earth, most living things use the same genetic code. However, different types of organisms show preferences for one or more codons that encode an amino acid. For example, human genes encode the amino acid alanine with the codon GCC four times more often than human genes use the alanine-encoding codon GCG. The preference for certain codons is called *codon bias*, and it affects protein synthesis. A cell produces proteins at a slower rate if messenger RNA contains rarely used codons.

Scientists exploited codon bias to design a new type of vaccine. They made mutant polioviruses with genomes that encoded poliovirus proteins using rare codons. These were silent mutations because the mutated genomes encode the same amino acid sequences as those encoded by normal genomes. The use of rare codons had an effect. The mutant viruses were less effective at causing infection in mice. Nevertheless, the mutant viruses stimulated the immune system. The method of customizing viral genes with rare codons could provide safer live vaccines against polio and other diseases.

provide immune protection for the upcoming flu season. The process does not always work. Production of a flu vaccine may require up to nine months. During this time, an antigenic drift may create a new virus strain. As a result, the vaccine would be out of date and have reduced effectiveness.

EMERGING VIRUSES

In January 2003, a young farmer from a South American village became ill. The disease began with a fever and a headache. Then the farmer's muscles and joints began to ache, and he started to lose blood. He died two weeks later. A local doctor sent tissue samples to the CDC for analysis. In 2008, CDC scientists reported that a new type of virus had infected the farmer. They named the virus *Chapare* after the farmer's home province. Scientists suggested that a rodent might be the natural host for the Chapare virus and that the virus happened to infect a human.

The appearance of new viral infections raises concern because drugs and vaccines may not be available to combat the infection. A new viral disease may be caused by an emerging virus. Emerging viruses are viruses that have recently infected a new host species, and/or appear in a new part of the world.

New Host Species

A number of viruses, like the Chapare virus, inflict human disease after switching host species. One famous emerging virus appeared in the Four Corners region of the United States, which consists of Utah, Arizona, Colorado, and New Mexico. Although the area is usually very dry, it experienced heavy rainfall and snowfall during the early 1990s. The wet weather increased the growth of piñon nuts, which is a major food source for deer mice. The well-fed animals reproduced. By 1993, the local deer mouse population had increased by at least tenfold. Many of the deer mice carried a virus that the mice excreted in their saliva, urine, and feces. Infected animals spread the virus to humans, who developed respiratory illnesses. Scientists found that the virus was a type of hantavirus that was not known to cause disease in humans. They almost dubbed the virus the "Four Corners virus." However, the people of Four Corners protested, fearing that the name might discourage tourists. So, the virus was named the *sin nombre virus*—"the virus without a name." The sin nombre virus has infected people throughout North and South America since its discovery in Four Corners.

In 2002, doctors treated patients with a new respiratory disease in southern China. During the next year, one of the doctors visited a Hong Kong hotel. He became sick and died. Guests of the hotel traveled around the world, unknowingly carrying the illness with them. An outbreak of a new viral disease called *severe acute*

Infectious Proteins and RNAs

In 1982, University of California scientist Stanley B. Prusiner reported his studies on the infectious agent that causes a central nervous system disorder in sheep called *scrapie*. He proposed that an infectious protein caused scrapie and that neither DNA nor RNA was involved in the spread of the disease. Prusiner called the protein a **prion**—proteinaceous infectious particle.

Studies have shown that all mammals have prion proteins in brain nerve cells. The prion proteins are called *prion protein-cellular* (PrPC). Normal PrPC proteins have a corkscrew shape. A cell usually discards any PrPC protein that flattens into an abnormal form of a prion called *prion protein-scrapie* (PrPSc). Sometimes, cells cannot get rid of the mangled PrPSc proteins, which form large masses, harm nerve cells, and injure the brain. Affected regions in a diseased brain become porous like a sponge. A person or animal with PrPSc proteins that build up in nerve cells shows signs of brain damage. Prion diseases often lead to death.

Certain genetic mutations in human prion protein genes may produce unstable forms of PrPC that unfold into the PrPSc form. Disease-causing PrPSc proteins also spread like typical viruses. Two well-known prion disorders are mad cow disease, known as Creutzfeldt-Jakob disease in humans. According to one theory, prion diseases spread because PrPSc proteins convert normal PrPC proteins into the abnormal PrPSc form. These new abnormal PrPSc proteins transform more normal PrPC proteins and so on. The ability to form new PrPSc proteins by this chain reaction spreads prion disease without the need for DNA or RNA.

A **viroid** is another type of infectious agent. Viroids are small, single-stranded, circular RNA molecules that infect

(continues)

(continued)

plants. Unlike viruses, viroids lack a capsid. These tiny RNA molecules cause at least 15 crop diseases that look like viral infections. Viroids reproduce in plant cells, and new viroids spread throughout the plant and spread to healthy plants. Scientists continue to investigate viroids to understand how they cause disease.

respiratory syndrome (SARS) had begun. About 20 countries reported cases within one month. Quarantine measures controlled the outbreak. By then, more than 8,000 people had become ill, and about 800 had died. Researchers suggest that the SARS virus crossed from animals into humans a number of times until one form of the virus gained mutations that allowed for human-to-human transmission.

After a virus enters a new species, it may evolve into a new virus. This viral evolution happened with the simian immunodeficiency virus. The virus usually infects nonhuman primates, such as chimpanzees, but the virus crossed the species barrier, infected humans, and mutated to a new virus called *human immunodeficiency virus* (HIV).

New Regions of the World

As the spread of the SARS virus shows, human activities accidently spread viruses. Airplane travel might have also caused the 1999 outbreak of the West Nile virus in New York City. One popular theory is that airplanes traveling from the African continent to the New York City area carried mosquitoes infected with the West Nile virus.

Global warming appears to be a major factor in the spread of the bluetongue virus, which causes the tongues of some animals to become swollen and blue. Biting insects spread the virus spread between hosts. For a long time, the virus had infected animals in Africa and the Middle East. In 1998, six strains of the virus began to spread north. By 2004, the virus had killed more than one million sheep in Europe. Because of warmer climates, the insect that transmits the virus has been moving north.

In 1967, laboratory workers developed a strange disease in the German town of Marburg. They had been working with organs and cell cultures from African green monkeys transported from Uganda. Seven of the laboratory workers died, and infection spread to hospital staff that cared for these workers. The monkeys had been infected with a virus now called the *Marburg virus.*

Reemerging Viruses

A reemerging virus is a rare virus that causes increasing numbers of infections. Monkeypox virus is an example of a reemerging virus. Rodents in Central and West Africa are the natural hosts for the virus. Once in a while, the virus infects monkeys, causing a disease similar to the human smallpox disease. In 2007, more than 700 rodents were shipped from West Africa to a pet distributor in the United States. The shipment included giant Gambian pouched rats that were infected with the monkeypox virus. The rodents were housed next to prairie dogs, which became infected. The infected prairie dogs were sold at an exotic pet swap meeting and transmitted the monkeypox virus to 71 people.

The United Kingdom had seen a decline in mumps and measles through the late 1990s. The disappearance of the diseases has been attributed to widespread vaccination. As public concerns arose about the safety of vaccines, fewer parents had their children vaccinated. As a result, measles and mumps reemerged. According to the Health Protection Agency in the United Kingdom, doctors now see thousands of mumps cases and hundreds of measles cases each year.

Challenges and Controversies

At the beginning of the twentieth century, infectious diseases caused most deaths worldwide. Improvements in hygiene and nutrition helped to combat these diseases. The development of antiviral drugs and vaccines for viral infections played a vital role in decreasing the spread of viral infections. By the 1960s, science appeared to have won the war against illnesses caused by viruses and bacteria. In 1969, U.S. Surgeon General William H. Stewart declared that it was time to close the book on infectious diseases. Scientists should focus research on treatments for heart disease, cancer, and other noninfectious disorders.

By the end of the twentieth century, scientists realized that they had been too optimistic. Old viruses reemerged, and new viruses appeared. One of the new viruses—human immunodeficiency virus-1 (HIV-1)—created a new pandemic.

HIV-1

Scientists first identified HIV during the early 1980s. There are two types of the virus. HIV-1 is mainly to blame for the acquired immune deficiency syndrome (AIDS) pandemic. The Joint United Nations Programme on HIV/AIDS reported that more than 33 million

Vaccination Programs Incite Controversies

When governments support vaccination programs, they create a conflict. Individuals must decide to give up some of their freedom to benefit the community. In the United Kingdom, an 1853 law required vaccination for all infants. Parents who broke the law faced a fine or prison. Riots erupted there, and protests occurred in the United States, as well. During the late nineteenth century, state governments tried to enforce vaccination laws and sparked the rise of anti-vaccination movements. Protestors fought in the streets and in the courts. Seven states withdrew their compulsory vaccination laws, leaving the decision about vaccination to individuals. An anti-vaccination movement continues to this day in the United States.

During the late 1990s, parents in the United States became concerned that an additive called *thimerosal* in vaccines may cause a disorder called *autism*, which impairs a person's social interaction and his or her ability to communicate. Thimerosal contains mercury, which helps to prevent the growth of bacteria in vaccines. Government agencies could find no evidence that the thimerosal in vaccines increases the risk of developing autism. Nevertheless, vaccine producers agreed to reduce or remove thimerosal from vaccines.

Despite government assurances, many parents fear that vaccines can cause their children to develop autism or other disorders. In an article entitled, "Vaccine Safety Concerns," the U.S. Centers for Disease Control and Prevention suggests that some parents may resist vaccination for their children against measles and other diseases because the diseases no longer appear to exist. After all, most parents today have not seen many childhood diseases that were very common at one time. In an article published in

(continues)

(continues)

the *American Journal of Public Health* (February 2008), Dr. Jeffrey Baker suggests that adverse media coverage and misinformation on the Internet contribute to the anxiety about vaccines.

This is not to say that concerns about vaccines lack any basis. In April 2008, the federal government decided that a nine-year-old girl had acquired an illness with autism symptoms as a result of vaccines she received as an infant. The vaccines appear to have made the girl's rare genetic condition worse. A small number of children may have genetic conditions that make them prone to adverse effects of vaccines. Research will be required to identify those children who may be at risk.

people live with an HIV infection. According to the National Institutes of Health, about 40,000 new HIV infections occur every year in the United States alone. About 10% to 20% of HIV-1 infected people develop AIDS within five years of infection. Others remain free of AIDS for 15 years or more.

An untreated HIV infection impairs the function of the immune system. The viruses kill CD4 cells, a type of white blood cell that has a CD4 protein in the cell membrane. The immune system needs CD4 cells to fight invading organisms. When the blood level of CD4 cells falls too low, a person becomes prone to infections from viruses, bacteria, and fungi. The impaired immune system also cannot defend the body against cancer.

HIV has an outer membrane envelope that covers the capsid. Spikelike viral proteins stick out from the envelope and allow the virus to enter a host cell. HIV is a retrovirus and carries an RNA genome inside the capsid. The genome encodes the capsid proteins and enzymes needed to make new viruses.

CD4 cells are the main host cells for HIV-1. When the virus finds its target cell, a viral protein binds with the cell's CD4 protein. The virus envelope and the cell membrane fuse, and the contents of the HIV

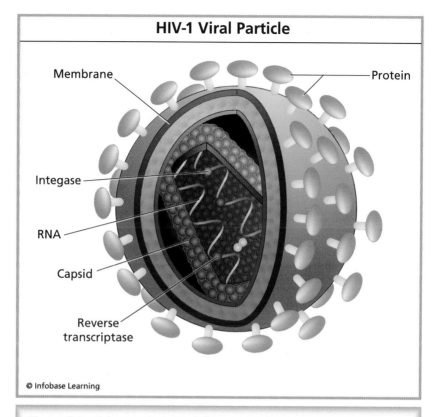

HIV-1 Viral Particle

Membrane

Protein

Integase

RNA

Capsid

Reverse
transcriptase

© Infobase Learning

Figure 9.1   A human immunodeficiency viral particle is covered by a
lipid bilayer from the host cell.

envelope are released into the cell's cytoplasm. Viral reverse transcriptase makes a DNA copy of the RNA genome, and the DNA molecule moves into the nucleus. A viral enzyme called *integrase* may insert the viral DNA into the host cell DNA. After insertion, a viral DNA molecule called a *provirus* may remain inactive for some time before stimulating new virus production. When the provirus becomes activated, messenger RNA is synthesized from viral DNA. The messenger RNA moves to the cell's protein synthesis machinery for the production of viral proteins. New HIV proteins and copies of HIV genomic RNA assemble into viruses. New viruses kill CD4 cells as they burst from the host cells. HIV-1 reproduces quickly as it spreads throughout the body. Several billion new viruses may be produced every day.

EFFORTS TO TREAT HIV INFECTIONS

Scientists have developed about 30 approved drugs for treating people infected with HIV. The drugs target four stages of the virus life cycle. Some drugs interfere with the fusion of the viral envelope and the cell membrane to prevent the virus from entering the host cell. Other drugs prevent reverse transcriptase from synthesizing DNA from the HIV genome, inhibit integrase to block the insertion of viral DNA into host cell DNA, or block an enzyme needed to make new infectious viruses. Antiviral drugs can reduce HIV to low levels in the body. People infected with HIV must always take drugs to hinder HIV reproduction; no drug can cure HIV infection.

The HIV pandemic continues. Scientists suggest that only a vaccine can control the spread of HIV. In 1984, U.S. secretary of Health

The Cow Pock __ or __ the Wonderful Effects of the New Inoculation! __ vide. the Publications of ye Anti Vaccine Society.

Figure 9.2 This 1802 parody of Dr. Jenner's cowpox vaccine reflects common controversies about vaccination. Jenner is pictured vaccinating a frightened woman, as cows emerge from different parts of people's bodies.

Controversy: Genetically Engineered Papayas

For decades, Hawaiian papaya farmers have struggled against papaya ringspot virus. The virus causes a disease that ruins papaya fruit with ringed spots and can kill papaya trees. Ringspot virus first appeared on Oahu Island during the 1940s and proceeded to wipe out one papaya farm after another. In the early 1960s, papaya growers tried to move their operations to the Puna district of Hawaii Island. Ringspot virus began to spread toward Puna. By 1994, the virus had infected more than half of the Puna crops. The Hawaii Department of Agriculture abandoned traditional methods to control the spread of ringspot virus.

Cornell University plant virus expert Dennis Gonsalves offered a way to help papaya farmers. He and his team had produced a genetically engineered (GE) papaya that synthesized a capsid protein of the ringspot virus. Unlike conventional papaya plants, the GE plants resisted ringspot virus infection. Gonsalves had based his GE papaya on the observation that a GE plant containing a virus capsid gene is protected against disease caused by the virus. It is unclear why healthy plants that make viral capsid proteins can resist infection. Possibly, cells that synthesize viral capsid proteins prevent an invading virus from shedding its capsid proteins. The genome of the viral invader becomes locked in its protein coat.

GE papayas have incited controversy in Hawaii. Some raised concerns about possible allergic reactions in people who eat papaya fruit containing viral capsid proteins. So far, tests have shown that an allergic reaction does not pose a significant risk. Protests against GE papaya also stem from the possibility of cross pollination. The fertilization of conventional papaya plants by the pollen of GE papayas would

(continues)

(continues)

result in fruits that produce seeds carrying the ringspot virus capsid gene. The seeds would mature into GE papaya trees. The contamination of a crop with GE papayas poses a problem for farmers of conventional papayas, particularly those who use organic agricultural methods. GE papayas are not considered organic produce. Ongoing studies suggest that contamination can be prevented by the adequate separation of GE papaya crops and conventional crops.

The genetic alteration of papaya is not unique. GE squash, grapes, plums, and sugar beets have also been altered to resist viral infections. Farmers are growing these GE crops for sale or in large-scale tests.

and Human Services Margaret Heckler predicted that an HIV vaccine would be available within two years. Twenty-five years have passed with no vaccine in sight.

HIV has characteristics that to date have thwarted researchers' efforts to design a vaccine to prevent infection or a drug to cure an infection. They include:

- HIV reproduces at a rapid rate during the entire course of an infection. New viruses are produced so quickly that a person who has had an infection for 10 years carries HIV with genomes 3,000 generations removed from the genomes of the viruses that started the infection.
- Like all retroviruses, HIV needs reverse transcriptase to make DNA copies of its RNA genome. Reverse transcriptase lacks the ability to proofread nucleotide sequences and correct errors. As a result, more than one-half of the new HIV genomes contain at least one error in the nucleotide sequence. Because of their rapid mutation rate, viruses develop a resistance to drugs. An antiviral drug works for a short period of time before HIV mutants appear. Mutations also change HIV antigens and can allow viruses to escape antibodies.

- After insertion into host cell DNA, the HIV provirus can remain dormant for a long time. Cells carrying inactive provirus become an HIV reservoir that allows the virus to escape detection by the immune system.
- Even an active provirus can dodge the immune system. An active provirus stimulates the production of a protein called *Nef.* The Nef protein removes molecules from host cell membranes that would signal an infection, thus protecting an infected cell from killer cells that would otherwise destroy the host cell before the infection is complete.

The high mutation rate of HIV presents a huge challenge to the design of a vaccine. To be effective, the vaccine must stimulate the immune system against antigens that quickly mutate from the antigens in the vaccine. HIV presents another problem for the design of a vaccine. The basis of vaccines is to prime immune system memory cells. Yet HIV destroys CD4 cells, which are one type of memory cell.

During 2007, doctors stopped a trial of an HIV vaccine in humans because the vaccine appeared to cause more harm than good. A 2008 test of another vaccine was canceled when it seemed that the vaccine would yield the same results. The invention of an HIV vaccine will require a thorough understanding of the immune system and perhaps the development of new recombinant DNA approaches to vaccine production.

THE BATTLE CONTINUES

In 1969, it might have seemed that science had defeated viral infections. But viruses have proved to be tougher and trickier than anticipated. As a group, viruses present a shifting target. Mutations ensure that viruses like HIV and the influenza virus evade attempts to make vaccines. Mutations also enable viruses to develop resistance to antiviral drugs. Another complication arises from the shifting pattern of viral diseases. New viruses emerge and old viruses reemerge. In addition, mutations enable viruses to jump from normal animal hosts to inflict new diseases in human hosts.

Scientists might find ways to finally defeat all viruses one day. For now, viruses remain pieces of bad news wrapped in proteins.

Glossary

adaptive immune system (adaptive immunity or specific immunity) Response of the immune system with antibodies and white blood cells that target viral antigens

amino acid The chemical building block of a protein

antibody A protein that binds with a substance foreign to a body

antigen A substance that the immune system recognizes as foreign

antigenic drift Minor changes in virus antigens

antigenic shift A major change in the antigens of a virus that can create a pandemic virus strain

antisense DNA or antisense RNA A DNA molecule or an RNA molecule with a nucleotide sequence that allows the formation of base pairs with a messenger RNA molecule

bacteria Microorganisms that reproduce themselves

base A molecule that forms part of DNA and RNA

base pair Two bases that are held together by weak bonds in a double-stranded DNA or RNA molecule

capsid A coat of proteins that surrounds a viral genome

chromosome A structure in a cell that contains DNA

codon A group of three nucleotides that code for an amino acid

complementary nucleotide sequences Nucleotide sequences of a single-stranded DNA molecule or a single-stranded RNA molecule that allow the single-stranded molecule to bind another single-stranded DNA or RNA by forming base pairs (for example, the DNA sequence GTTACA is complementary to the DNA sequence CAATGT)

cytoplasm A cell's cytosol and organelles found outside the nucleus

deoxyribonucleic acid (DNA) A nucleic acid molecule that encodes genetic information and contains deoxyribose sugar

endoplasmic reticulum A system of membranes in the cytoplasm and a site of protein synthesis

epidemic The occurrence of a high number of cases of a similar illness in a region

gene A nucleotide sequence that encodes a protein or a functional RNA molecule

genetic code The collection of 64 codons that specify 20 amino acids and the signals for stopping protein synthesis

genome The complete nucleotide sequences of an individual or species

Golgi bodies Collection of disk-shaped cytoplasmic organelles that transport protein

innate immune system (innate immunity or nonspecific immunity) An inborn (hard-wired) group of immune defenses against toxins and infectious agents identified as foreign to the body.

lysosomes Cellular organelles that digest waste products created by the cell and debris that travels inside the cell

messenger RNA An RNA molecule that transmits genetic information from DNA to a cell's protein-making apparatus

mitochondria Cellular organelles that process molecules obtained from food to supply energy to the cell

mitosis A type of cell division that produces two identical daughter cells

mutation A change in the nucleotide sequence of a DNA molecule or a change in the amino acid sequence of a protein

nucleotide The monomer of DNA that contains a sugar molecule, a chemical group that contains phosphorus, and a base

nucleus The organelle that contains most of a cell's DNA

pandemic A worldwide epidemic

parasite   Something that must live in or on a cell or organism

polymer   A large chemical made by combining smaller units

prion   An infectious protein

protein   A polymer of amino acids

recombinant DNA   DNA that has been altered in the lab by the addition or deletion of nucleotide sequences

reservoir   A type of organism in which a virus normally lives and reproduces

retrovirus   A virus with an RNA genome

reverse transcriptase   An enzyme carried by retroviruses to synthesize DNA from a viral RNA genome

ribonucleic acid (RNA)   A nucleic acid molecule that can encode genetic information and contains ribose sugar

RNA interference (RNAi)   A process that decreases or blocks protein synthesis

transcription   The process of making an RNA copy of a DNA nucleotide sequence

translation   The process of making a protein using genetic code information in messenger RNA

vaccine   A material that stimulates the immune system

vector   An organism, such as an insect, that transmits viruses

viroid   An infectious RNA molecule that causes plant diseases

virus   An infectious agent that consists of a DNA or RNA genome, a protein capsid, and sometimes a membrane envelope that surrounds the capsid

white blood cell   A cell of the immune system that attacks foreign bacteria and viruses

Bibliography

Abid, K. and C. Soto. "The Intriguing Prion Disorders," *Cellular and Molecular Life Sciences* 63 (2006): 2342–2351.

Aguzzi, Adriano, Christina Sigurdson, and Mathias Heikenwaelder. "Molecular Mechanisms of Prion Pathogenesis," *Annual Review of Pathology* 3 (2008): 11–40.

Allen, Arthur. *Vaccine: The Controversial Story of Medicine's Greatest Lifesaver*. New York, NY: W.W. Norton & Company, 2007.

American Cancer Society. *Cancer Facts & Figures 2008*. Atlanta, GA: American Cancer Society, 2008.

Anderson, B.J. "Managing Herpes Gladiatorum Outbreaks in Competitive Wrestling: The 2007 Minnesota Experience," *Current Sports Medicine Reports* 7 (2008): 323–327.

Andersson, Jan. "HIV after 25 Years: How to Induce a Vaccine?" *Journal of Internal Medicine* 263 (2008): 215–217.

Aslam, M.A., F.R. Awan, I. Tauseef, S. Ali, N. Ahmad, N.A. Malik, M.N. Riaz et al. "Identification of Hepatitis B Virus Core Mutants by PCR-RFLP in Chronic Hepatitis B Patients from Punjab, Pakistan," *Archives of Virology* 153 (2008): 163–170.

Avila, Maria, Najwane Saïd, and David M. Ojcius. "The Book Reopened on Infectious Diseases," *Microbes and Infection* 10 (2008): 942–947.

Baden, Lindsey, R. and Raphael Dolin. "Antiviral Chemotherapy, Excluding Antiretroviral Drugs," In *Harrison's Principles of Internal Medicine*, 16th ed., edited by Dennis L. Kasper, Eugene Braunwald, Anthony S. Fauci, Stephen L. Hauser, Dan L. Longo, and J. Larry Jameson, 1027–1035. New York, NY: The McGraw-Hill Companies, Inc., 2005.

Baker, Jeffrey P. "Mercury, Vaccines, and Autism," *American Journal of Public Health* 98 (2008): 244–253.

Ban, Fumihiko, Satoe Asano, Shigeru Ozawa, Hiroyuki Eda, James Norman, William G. Stroop, and Kazuo Yanagi. "Analysis of Herpes Simplex Virus Type 1 Restriction Fragment Length Polymorphism Variants

Associated with Herpes Gladiatorum and Kaposi's Varicelliform Eruption in Sumo Wrestlers," *Journal of General Virology* 89 (2008): 2410–2415.

Baulcombe, David C. "Mechanisms of Pathogen-Derived Resistance to Viruses in Transgenic Plants," *The Plant Cell* 8 (1996): 1833–1844.

Bennett, Simeon. "Nobel Winner Sees Potential for Flu-Carrying Bacteria in Food." Available online at http://www.bloomberg.com. Accessed on February 16, 2011.

Borden, Ernest C., Ganes C. Sen, Gilles Uze, Robert H. Silverman, Richard M. Ransohoff, Graham R. Foster, and George R. Stark. "Interferons at Age 50: Past, Current and Future Impact on Biomedicine," *Nature Reviews Drug Discovery* 6 (2007): 975–990.

Brault, Aaron C., Claire Y-H Huang, Stanley A. Langevin, Richard M. Kinney, Richard A. Bowen, Wanichaya N. Ramey, Nicholas A. Panella et al. "A Single Positively Selected West Nile Viral Mutation Confers Increased Virogenesis in American Crows," *Nature Genetics* 39 (2007): 1162–1166.

Bren, Linda. "Bacteria-Eating Virus Approved as Food Additive," *U.S. Food and Drug Administration Consumer Magazine*, January 2007–February 2007. Available online at http://www.fda.gov. Accessed on June 17, 2008.

Bunkall, Alistair. "Zoo Pioneers Blood Sucking Bug." Available online at http://news.sky.com. Accessed on February 16, 2011.

Cabral, Ana Lucia B., Kil S. Lee, and Vilma R. Martins. "Regulation of the Cellular Prion Protein Gene Expression Depends on Chromatin Conformation," *Journal of Biological Chemistry* 277 (2002): 5675–5682.

Cann, Alan J. *Principles of Molecular Virology*, 4th ed.. New York, NY: Academic Press, Inc. (2005).

Cannell, John J., Michael Zasloff, Cedric F. Garland, Robert Scragg, and Edward Giovannucci. "On the Epidemiology of Influenza," *Virology Journal* 5 (February 5, 2008). Available online at http://www.virologyj.com/content/5/1/29. Accessed on February 16, 2011.

Carrat, F. and A. Flahault. "Influenza Vaccine: The Challenge of Antigenic Drift," *Vaccine* 25 (2007): 6852–6862.

Carter, John and Venetia Saunders. *Virology: Principles and Applications*. West Sussex, England: John Wiley & Sons, Ltd., 2007.

Castello, John D., Scott O. Rogers, William T. Starmer, Catharine M. Catranis, Lijun Ma, George D. Bachand, Yinghao Zhao et al. "Detection of Tomato Mosaic Tobamovirus RNA in Ancient Glacial Ice," *Polar Biology* 22 (1999): 207–212.

Chen, Yong, Guofeng Cheng, and Ram I. Mahato. "RNAi for Treating Hepatitis B Viral Infection," *Pharmaceutical Research* 25 (2008): 72–86.

Cohen, Mitchell L. "Changing Patterns of Infectious Disease," *Nature* 406 (2000): 762–767.

Coleman, J. Robert, Dimitris Papamichail, Steven Skiena, Bruce Futcher, Eckard Wimmer, and Steffen Mueller. "Virus Attenuation by Genome-Scale Changes in Codon Pair Bias," *Science* 320 (2008): 1784–1787.

Collinge, John and Anthony R. Clarke. "A General Model of Prion Strains and Their Pathogenicity," *Science* 318 (2007): 930–936.

Crawford, Dorothy H. *The Invisible Enemy: A Natural History of Viruses.* New York, NY: Oxford University Press, 2000.

De Clercq, Erik. "Antivirals and Antiviral Strategies," *Nature Reviews Microbiology* 2 (2004): 704–720.

———. "The Design of Drugs for HIV and HCV," *Nature Reviews Drug Discovery* 6 (2007): 1001–1018.

De Jesus, Nidia H. "Epidemics to Eradication: The Modern History of Poliomyelitis," *Virology Journal* 4 (2007). Available online at http://www.virologyj.com/content/4/1/70. Accessed on February 16, 2011.

Devlin, Thomas M., ed. *Textbook of Biochemistry with Clinical Correlations,* 4th ed. New York, NY: Wiley-Liss, Inc., 1997.

Dewannieux, Marie, Francis Harper, Aurélien Richaud, Claire Letzelter, David Ribet, Gérard Pierron, and Thierry Heidmann. "Identification of an Infectious Progenitor for the Multiple-Copy HERV-K Human Endogenous Retroelements," *Genome Research* 16 (2006): 1548–1556.

Ding, Biao and Asuka Itaya. "Viroid: A Useful Model for Studying the Basic Principles of Infection and RNA Biology," *Molecular Plant-Microbe Interactions* 20 (2007): 7–20.

El Sahly, Hanna M. and Wendy A. Keitel. "Pandemic H5N1 Influenza Vaccine Development: An Update," *Expert Review of Vaccines* 7 (2008): 241–247.

Enserink, Martin. "'Biased' Viruses Suggest New Vaccine Strategy for Polio and Other Diseases," *Science* 320 (2008): 1709.

"Epidemiologic Notes and Reports Herpes Gladiatorum at a High School Wrestling Camp—Minnesota," *Morbidity Mortality Weekly Report* 39 (1990): 69–71.

Flores, Ricardo, Carmen Hernández, A. Emilio Martínez de Alba, José-Antonio Daròs, and Francesco Di Serio. "Viroids and Viroid-Host Interactions," *Annual Review of Phytopathology* 43 (2005):117–139.

"Food Safety." Available online at http://www.intralytix.com. Accessed on February 16, 2011.

Fox, Jeffrey L. "Antivirals Become a Broader Enterprise," *Nature Biotechnology* 25 (2007): 1395–1402.

Fuchs, Marc and Dennis Gonsalves. "Safety of Virus-Resistant Transgenic Plants Two Decades after Their Introduction: Lessons from Realistic Field Risk Assessment Studies," *Annual Review of Phytopathology* 45 (2007): 173–202.

Gilbert, C. and G. Boivin. "Human Cytomegalovirus Resistance to Antiviral Drugs," *Antimicrobial Agents and Chemotherapy* 49 (2005): 873–883.

Ginsburg, Janet. "Virus Traps: Weapons of Mass Deception," *New Scientist,* No. 2626 (2007): 43–45.

Glick, Bernard R. and Jack J. Pasternak. *Molecular Biotechnology,* 3rd ed. Washington, D.C.: ASM Press, 2003.

"Global Polio Eradication." Available online at http://www.cdc.gov. Accessed on February 16, 2011.

Gonsalves, Dennis. "Control of Papaya Ringspot Virus in Papaya: A Case Study," *Annual Review of Phytopathology* 36 (1998): 415–437.

Griffiths, Anthony J.F., Susan R. Wessler, Richard C. Lewontin, and Sean B. Carroll. *Introduction to Genetic Analysis,* 9th ed. New York, NY: W.H. Freeman and Company, 2008.

Haasnoot, Joost, Ellen M. Westerhout, and Ben Berkhout. "RNA Interference Against Viruses: Strike and Counterstrike," *Nature Biotechnology* 25 (2007): 1435–1443.

Hagens, Steven and Mark L. Offerhaus. "Bacteriophages—New Weapons for Food Safety," *Food Technology* 62 (2008): 46–54.

Hankinson, Jessica. "Designing Foods to Prevent Diseases." Available online at http://www.worldandi.com. Accessed on June 10, 2008.

Harappanabally, Gita V., Christine L. Trask, and David E. Mandelbaum. "Vaccines and Autism: An Update," *Medicine & Health Rhode Island* 90 (2007): 308–310.

Hartwell, Leland H., Leroy Hood, Michael L. Goldberg, Ann E. Reynolds, Lee M. Silver, and Ruth C. Veres. *Genetics: From Genes to Genomes,* 3rd ed. New York, NY: McGraw-Hill, 2008.

Hilleman, Maurice R. "Vaccines in Historic Evolution and Perspective: A Narrative of Vaccine Discoveries," *Vaccine* 18 (2000): 1436–1447.

Hogle, James M. "Poliovirus Cell Entry: Common Structural Themes in Viral Cell Entry Pathways," *Annual Review of Microbiology* 56 (2002): 677–702.

Hu, Wei, Bernd Kieseier, Elliot Frohman, Todd N. Eagar, Roger N. Rosenberg, Hans-Peter Hartung , and Olaf Stüve. "Prion Proteins: Physiological Functions and Role in Neurological Disorders," *Journal of the Neurological Sciences* 264 (2008): 1–8.

"Intralytix, Inc., FAQ." Intralytix, Inc. Web Site. Available online at http://www.intralytix.com. Accessed on February 16, 2011.

Janeway, Charles A., Paul Travers, Mark Walport, and Mark Shlomchik. *Immunobiology*, 5th ed. New York, NY: Garland Publishing, 2001.

Kallings, L.O. "The First Postmodern Pandemic: 25 Years of HIV/AIDS," *Journal of Internal Medicine* 263 (2008): 218–243.

Kates, J.R. and McAuslan, B.R. "Poxvirus DNA-dependant RNA Polymerase," *Proceedings of the National Academy of Science, USA* 58 (1967): 134-141.

Kennedy, Michael T. *A Brief History of Disease, Science & Medicine*. Mission Viejo, CA: Asklepiad Press, 2004.

Khamsi, Roxanne. "Paralyzing Virus a Suspect in Disappearing Bee Mystery." Available online at http://www.newscientist.com. Accessed on February 16, 2011.

Kovacs, Gabor G. and Herbert Budka. "Prion Diseases: From Protein to Cell Pathology," *The American Journal of Pathology* 172 (2008): 555–565.

Kuypers, Jane, Nancy Wright, James Ferrenberg, Meei-Li Huang, Anne Cent, Lawrence Corey, and Rhoda Morrow. "Comparison of Real-Time PCR Assays with Fluorescent-Antibody Assays for Diagnosis of Respiratory Virus Infections in Children," *Journal of Clinical Microbiology* 44 (2006): 2382–2388.

Le Guenno, Bernard. "Emerging Viruses," *Scientific American* 273 (October 1995): 56–64.

Littler, Eddy and Bo Oberg. "Achievements and Challenges in Antiviral Drug Discovery," *Antiviral Chemistry & Chemotherapy* 16 (2005): 155–168.

Lim, Yong-beom, Eunji Lee, You-Rim Yoon, Myeong Sup Lee, and Myongsoo Lee. "Filamentous Artificial Virus from a Self-Assembled Discrete Nanoribbon," *Angewandte Chemie* 47 (2008): 4525–4528.

Liu, M.A. "DNA Vaccines: A Review," *Journal of Internal Medicine* 253 (2003): 402–410.

MacKenzie, Deborah. "Bloodsucking Bugs Help Vaccinate Flighty Zoo Animals," *New Scientist* 2659 (2008): 14.

Magner, Lois N. *A History of Medicine*, 2nd ed. New York, NY: Taylor & Francis, 2005.

Mahony, James B. "Detection of Respiratory Viruses by Molecular Methods," *Clinical Microbiology Reviews* 21 (2008): 716–747.

Masters, John R. "HeLa Cells 50 Years On: The Good, the Bad and the Ugly," *Nature Reviews Cancer* 2 (2002): 315–319.

"Measles Mortality Reduction and Regional Global Measles Elimination." Available online at http://www.cdc.gov. Accessed on June 6, 2008.

Moghadas, Seyed M., Christopher S. Bowman, Gergely Röst, and Jianhong Wu. "Population-Wide Emergence of Antiviral Resistance during Pandemic Influenza," *PLoS One* 3 (March 19, 2008). Available online at http://plosone.org. Accessed on February 16, 2011.

Mueller, Steffen, Dimitris Papamichail, J. Robert Coleman, Steven Skiena, and Eckard Wimmer. "Reduction of the Rate of Poliovirus Protein Synthesis Through Large-Scale Codon Deoptimization Causes Attenuation of Viral Virulence by Lowering Specific Infectivity," *Journal of Virology* 80 (2006): 9687–9696.

Münger, Karl, Amy Baldwin, Kirsten M. Edwards, Hiroyuki Hayakawa, Christine L. Nguyen, Michael Owens, Miranda Grace et al. "Mechanisms of Human Papillomavirus-Induced Oncogenesis," *Journal of Virology* 78 (2004): 11451–11460.

Norrby, Erling. "Yellow Fever and Max Theiler: The Only Nobel Prize for a Virus Vaccine," *Journal of Experimental Medicine* 204 (2007): 2779–2784.

———. "Nobel Prizes and the Emerging Virus Concept," *Archives of Virology* 153 (2008): 1109–1123.

Offit, Paul A. "Vaccines and Autism Revisited—The Hannah Poling Case," *The New England Journal of Medicine* 358 (2008): 2089–2091.

Oldstone, Michael B.A. *Viruses, Plagues, & History.* New York, NY: Oxford University Press, 1998.

Özduman Koray, Guido Wollmann, Joseph M Piepmeier, Anthony N. van den Pol. "Systemic Vesicular Stomatitis Virus Selectively Destroys Multifocal Glioma and Metastatic Carcinoma in Brain," *Journal of Neuroscience* 28 (2008): 1882–1893.

Park, Alice. "How Safe Are Vaccines?" *Time Magazine* (May 21, 2008). Available online at http://www.time.com. Accessed on Febrary 16, 2011.

Pekosz, Andrew and Gregory E. Glass. "Emerging Viral Diseases," *Maryland Medicine* 9 (2008): 11–16.

Pennazio, Sergio. "Genetics and Virology: Two Interdisciplinary Branches of Biology," *Rivista di Biologia/Biology Forum* 100 (2007): 119–146.

Procop, Gary W. "Molecular Diagnostics for the Detection and Characterization of Microbial Pathogens," *Clinical Infectious Diseases* 45 (2007): S99–S111.

Pungpapong, Surakit, W. Ray Kim, and John J. Poterucha. "Natural History of Hepatitis B Virus Infection: An Update for Clinicians," *Mayo Clinical Proceedings* 82 (2007): 967-975.

Quinton, Sarah "Tasty Ways to Replace Jabs," *Countryman*, June 19, 2008.

Randall, Richard E. and Stephen Goodbourn. "Interferons and Viruses: An Interplay Between Induction, Signalling, Antiviral Responses and Virus Countermeasures," *Journal of General Virology* 89 (2008): 1–47.

"Research Continues as Honey Bee Losses Rise in U.S., Fall in PA." Available online at http://aginfo.psu.edu/news/2008/5/beeresearch.html. Accessed on June 7, 2008.

Rivers, Thomas M. "Viruses and Koch's Postulates," *Journal of Bacteriology* 33 (1937): 1–12.

Rockoff, Jonathan D. and Hanah Cho. "U.S. OKs Spray to Kill Food Bacteria," *The Baltimore Sun*, August 19, 2006.

Rosenthal, Elisabeth. "As Earth Warms Up, Tropical Virus Moves to Italy," *The New York Times*, December 23, 2007.

Rossi, John J., Carl H. June, and Donald B. Kohn. "Genetic Therapies Against HIV," *Nature Biotechnology* 25 (2007): 1444–1454.

Samuel, Charles E. "Antiviral Actions of Interferons," *Clinical Microbiology Reviews* 14 (2001): 778–809.

Schaefer, Malinda R. Elizabeth R. Wonderlich, Jeremiah F. Roeth, Jolie A. Leonard, and Kathleen L. Collins. "HIV-1 Nef Targets MHC-I and CD4 for Degradation via a Final Common β-COP–Dependent Pathway in T Cells," *PLoS Pathogens* 4 (August 2008). Available online at http://www.plospathogens.org. Accessed on February 16, 2011.

Scott, Gillian M., Adriana Weinberg, William D. Rawlinson, and Sunwen Chou. "Multidrug Resistance Conferred by Novel DNA Polymerase Mutations in Human Cytomegalovirus Isolates," *Antimicrobial Agents and Chemotherapy* 51 (2007): 89–94.

Shors, T. *Understanding Viruses*. Sudbury, MA: Jones and Bartlett Publishers, 2009.

Skloot, Rebecca. "Henrietta's Dance," *John Hopkins Magazine* (April 2000). Available online at http://www.jhu.edu/jhumag/. Accessed on February 16, 2011.

Smith, Alicia E. and Ari Helenius. "How Viruses Enter Animal Cells," *Science* 304 (2004): 237–242.

Smith, Van. "Wonder Woman," *Baltimore City Paper*, April 17, 2002.

Spruance, Spotswood L. "Viral Infections," In *The Merck Manual of Medical Information*, 2nd Home Edition, edited by Mark H. Beers, 1154–1167. Whitehouse Station, NJ: Merck Research Laboratories, 2003.

Stang, Alexander, Klaus Korn, Oliver Wildner, and Klaus Überla. "Characterization of Virus Isolates by Particle-Associated Nucleic Acid PCR," *Journal of Clinical Microbiology* 43 (2005): 716–720.

Stevenson, Mario. "Can HIV be Cured?" *Scientific American* 299 (November 2008): 78–83.

Stokstad, Erik. "GM Papaya Takes on Ringspot Virus and Wins," *Science* 320 (2008): 472.

Strange, Richard N. and Peter R. Scott. "Plant Disease: A Threat to Global Food Security," *Annual Review of Phytopathology* 43(2005): 83–116.

Sullivan, Veronica, Karen K. Biron, Christine Talarico, Sylvia C. Stanat, Michelle Davis, Luann M. Pozzi, and Donald M. Coen. "A Point Mutation in the Human Cytomegalovirus DNA Polymerase Gene Confers Resistance to Ganciclovir and Phosphonylmethoxyalkyl Derivatives," *Antimicrobial Agents and Chemotherapy* 37 (1993): 19–25.

Susser, Mervyn, and Ezra Susser. "Choosing a Future for Epidemiology: I. Eras and Paradigms," *American Journal of Public Health* 86 (1996): 668–673.

Switzer, William M., Danuta Pieniazek, Priscilla Swanson, Helvi H. Samdal, Vinvent Soriano, Rima F. Khabbaz, Jonathan E Kaplan et al. "Phylogenetic Relationship and Geographic Distribution of Multiple Human T-cell Lymphotropic Virus Type II Subtypes," *Journal of Virology* 69 (1995): 621–632.

Taubenberger Jeffery K., Ann H. Reid, and Thomas G. Fanning. "Capturing a Killer Flu Virus," *Scientific American* 292 (2005): 62–71.

Taubenberger Jeffery K., Johan V. Hultin, and David M. Morens. "Discovery and Characterization of the 1918 Pandemic Influenza Virus in Historical Context," *Antiviral Therapy* 12 (2007): 581–591.

"The Deadly Dozen: The Wildlife Conservation Society Sounds the Alarm on Wildlife-Human Disease Threats in the Age of Climate Change." Available online at http://www.wcs.org . Accessed on February 16, 2011.

Understanding Vaccines. National Institutes of Health Publication No. 08-4219 (January 2008).

Vaughn, David W., Ananda Nisalak, Tom Solomon, Siripen Kalayanarooj, Nguyen Minh Dung, Rachel Kneen, Andrea Cuzzubbo et al. "Rapid Serologic Diagnosis of Dengue Virus Infection Using a Commercial Capture ELISA That Distinguishes Primary and Secondary Infections," *American Journal of Tropical Medicine and Hygiene* 60 (1999): 693–698.

"Virus Makes Honeybees Mean," *New Scientist* 2432 (2004): 16.

Von Itzstein, Mark. "The War Against Influenza: Discovery and Development of Sialidase Inhibitors," *Nature Reviews Drug Discovery* 6 (2007): 967–974.

Walker, Bruce D., and Dennis R. Burton. "Toward an AIDS Vaccine," *Science* 320 (2008): 760–764.

Walker, Matt. "Back from the Dead," *New Scientist* 2202 (1999): 4.

Wang, Fred and Elliott Kieff. "Medical Virology," In *Harrison's Principles of Internal Medicine*, 16th ed., edited by Dennis L. Kasper, Eugene Braunwald, Anthony S. Fauci, Stephen L. Hauser, Dan L. Longo, and J. Larry Jameson, 1019–1027. New York, NY: The McGraw-Hill Companies, Inc., 2005.

Watkins, David I. "The Vaccine Search Goes On," *Scientific American* 299 (November 2008): 69–74 and 76.

Watson, James D., Amy A. Caudy, Richard M. Myers, and Jan A. Witkowski. *Recombinant DNA: Genes and Genomes—A Short Course*, 3rd ed. New York, NY: W.H. Freeman and Company, 2007.

Willoughby, R.E., Jr. "A Cure for Rabies?" *Scientific American* 296 (2007): 88–95.

Winther, Birgit, Karen McCue, Kathleen Ashe, Joseph R. Rubino, and J. Owen Hendley. "Environmental Contamination with Rhinovirus and Transfer to Fingers of Healthy Individuals by Daily Life Activity," *Journal of Medical Virology* 79 (2007): 1606–1610.

Wolfe, Robert M. and Lisa K Sharp. "Anti-Vaccinationists Past and Present," *British Medical Journal* 325 (2002): 430–432.

Yoon, Carol Kaesuk. "Controversy over GE Virus-Spliced Hawaiian Papayas," *The New York Times*, July 20, 1999.

Zimmer, Carl. "Scientists Explore Ways to Lure Viruses to Their Death," *The New York Times*, March 27, 2007.

Further Resources

Books

Alter, Judy. *Vaccines*. Ann Arbor, MI: Cherry Lake Publishing, 2008.

Boudreau, Gloria. *The Immune System*. San Diego, CA: KidHaven Press, 2004.

Claybourne, Anna. *Introduction to Genes and DNA*. London, England: Usborne Publishing Limited, 2003.

Emmer, Richard. *Virus Hunter*. New York, NY: Chelsea House Publishers, 2005.

Fridell, Ron. *Decoding Life: Unraveling the Mysteries of the Genome*. Minneapolis, MN: Lerner Publishing Group, 2004.

Marrin, Albert. *Dr. Jenner and the Speckled Monster: The Discovery of the Smallpox Vaccine*. New York, NY: Dutton Juvenile, 2002.

Phelan, Glen. *Double Helix*. Washington, D.C.: National Geographic Children's Books, 2006.

Sfakianos, Jeffrey N. *West Nile Virus*. New York, NY: Chelsea House Publishers, 2004.

Storad, Conrad J. *Inside AIDS: HIV Attacks the Immune System*. Minneapolis, MN: Lerner Publications, 1998.

Walker, Richard. *Genes and DNA*. New York, NY: Houghton Mifflin Company, 2003.

Web Sites

Access Excellence at the National Health Museum
http://www.accessexcellence.org/
> *The National Health Museum offers general information and images about viruses and molecular biology.*

All the Virology of the WWW

http://www.virology.net/garryfavweb.html

> *The Web site offers a large number of links to information about viruses on the Internet, including sites on virology courses, plant viruses, antiviral drugs, and viruses in the news.*

DNA from the Beginning

http://www.dnaftb.org

> *The Cold Spring Harbor Laboratory offers information on DNA, RNA, genes, mutations, and viruses.*

Emerging Infectious Diseases

http://www.cdc.gov/ncidod/EID/index.htm

> *The U.S. Centers for Disease Control and Prevention publishes an online journal that tracks the latest developments in the field of emerging viruses.*

Vaccines and Immunizations

http://www.cdc.gov/vaccines/

> *The U.S. Centers for Disease Control and Prevention offers a wealth of information on vaccines, including vaccine basics, vaccine laws, and advice to parents about vaccinations.*

Viruses: From Structure to Biology

http://virologyhistory.wustl.edu/index.htm

> *This Web site presents a history of the discovery of viruses and details important viruses, such as the polio and influenza viruses.*

Picture Credits

Index

Medawar, Peter and Jane, 30
memory cells, 86, 117
messenger RNA (mRNA), 24, 79, 99–100
Mexican kissing bugs, 89
miasma theory of disease, 7–8, 10
micro-RNAs, 79
missense mutations, 100, 102
mitochondria, 17
mitosis, 53–55
monkeypox virus, 109
monolayer cell cultures, 59
mosquitoes, 22–23, 44–46, 96, 97
mumps, 109
mutations, 62, 97–105, 116

N

N protein (neuramidase), 75–76, 90, 102–104
naked viruses, 35
natural killer cells, 49
necrosis, 39
Nelmes, Sarah, 84, 85
nematodes, as vectors of plant viruses, 44
neuramidase (N protein), 75–76, 90, 102–104
nonsense codons, 99
nonsense mutations, 100
nonspecific immune response, 49–50
nuclei, 18
nucleocapsid, 31–32, 33
nucleotides, 19–21, 64–67, 74–75, 97–102

O

organelles, 17
oseltamivir, 76

P

pandemics, 52, 102–104, 110
papaya ringspot viruses, 115–116
papillomaviruses, 55–56
parasites, viruses as, 12

Pasteur, Louis, 10, 84
PCR (polymerase chain reaction), 64–67
perforins, 50
petunias, 78
phages, 11, 40, 41–43
phagocyte cells, 49
Phipps, James, 84
plant viruses, 38–39, 44, 46, 115–116. *See also Specific viruses*
plasmodesmata, 38–39
plug drugs, 75–76
polioviruses, 11, 61, 81, 90–92, 105
pollination, 28
polymers, 18–19
poxviruses, 32
prairie dogs, 109
primers, 64–65
Pringle, John, 9
prions, 107
proteins, 11, 17, 23–29, 30–32
proviruses, 40, 117
Prusiner, Stanley B., 107

R

rabies, 84, 90
real-time PCR, 66–67
recombinant DNA technology, 87
recombinant virus vaccines, 87–89
red blood cells, 70
Reed, Walter, 95
reemerging viruses, 109
replication of viruses, 16, 33–36, 37, 116
reservoir hosts, 46, 117
resistance, 49–50, 73
respiratory syncytial virus (RSV), 81
restriction enzymes, 67–68, 71
restriction fragment length polymorphism (RFLP), 67–71
retroviruses, 37, 40, 75, 116
reverse transcriptase, 37, 64, 116

RFLP (restriction fragment length polymorphism), 67–71
rhinoviruses, 47–48, 51
ribose sugars, 24
ringspot virus, 115–116
RISC (RNA-induced silencing complex), 79
RNA (ribonucleic acid), 11, 12–14, 24–26, 32–33, 64–67, 107–108
RNA polymerase, 24–25
RNA viruses, 36–40
RNAi (RNA interference) therapy, 78–82
RNA-induced silencing complex (RISC), 79
RNA-like strand of DNA, 25
rodents, 46–47, 106, 109
roundworms, 78–79
RSV (respiratory syncytial virus), 81
rugby, 14
Russian Flu, 104

S

Sabin, Albert, 92
Salk, Jonas, 91–92
sanitation, 8
SARS (severe acute respiratory syndrome), 106–108
scrapie, 107
scrumpox, 14
sense strand, 25
sense strand RNA genomes, 32
serological detection methods, 61–63
severe acute respiratory syndrome (SARS), 106–108
sheep, 89, 108
shingles, 52–53
silent mutations, 100, 101, 105
sin nombre virus, 106
small interfering RNAs (siRNAs), 79–82
smallpox, 83–84, 92–93, 109

About the Author

Phill Jones earned a Ph.D. in physiology and pharmacology from the University of California at San Diego. After completing postdoctoral training at the Stanford University School of Medicine, he joined the Department of Biochemistry at the University of Kentucky Medical Center as an assistant professor. Here, he taught classes in molecular biology and medicine and researched aspects of gene expression. He later earned a JD at the University of Kentucky College of Law and worked for 10 years as a patent attorney, specializing in biological, chemical, and medical inventions. Dr. Jones is now a full-time writer. His articles have appeared in *Today's Science on File, The World Almanac and Book of Facts, History Magazine, Forensic Magazine, Genomics and Proteomics Magazine, Encyclopedia of Forensic Science, The Science of Michael Crichton, Forensic Nurse Magazine, Nature Biotechnology, Information Systems for Biotechnology News Report, Law and Order Magazine, PharmaTechnology Magazine,* and Florida Department of Education publications. His books, *Sickle Cell Disease* (2008), and *The Genetic Code* (2010) were published by Chelsea House. He also wrote and teaches an online course in forensic science for writers.